CUTHBERT
The Valley That Time Forgot

#10

by

Patrick Barrett

A Wild Wolf Publication

Published by Wild Wolf Publishing in 2016
Copyright © 2016 Patrick Barrett

First print

All characters appearing in this work are fictitious. Any resemblance to real persons, living or dead, is purely coincidental.

ISBN: 978-1-907954-59-7
Also available as an e-book

www.wildwolfpublishing.com

Dedicated to my beautiful wife Paula, without whom these books would never have seen the light of day. The theme of this book was suggested by my dinosaur mad grand-son, Adam.

Chapter One

The scream came from the far end of the Valley, the place the real Valley folk referred to as 'The old end' which was a bit odd because the Valley must have all been the same age from the day someone obtained planning permission for it.

The echo reverberated along the Valley and the different genders reacted quite differently to it, the men struck heroic poses and glanced at each other hoping that someone else would go and investigate whilst the women paused for a moment before Marjorie shrugged and said, "Geraldine's found something."

Geraldine had in fact found something, something which must be kept secret at all costs which was unfortunate because her scream of excitement had alerted the Valley mafia who had dispatched scouts in all directions and even worse than that for secrecy, who should be in the vicinity but Percy.

* * *

Cuthbert sat at the ancient table in his kitchen and stared at the space where his friend Percy should be.

Percy wasn't just a friend; or a companion or another heartbeat around the house, he was a presence. When Percy was around, the whole Valley held its breath in case someone made a mistake and inspired him to regale them with tales of his ancestors who had apparently saved the world many times and repelled every mythical invader to ever threaten these shores.

Cuthbert sighed; at last he had something to brag about, he had finished a jigsaw puzzle in nine months when it said between four and seven years on the box, but as usual with Cuthbert's successes, there was no-one to share it with.

* * *

Percy was definitely up to something, he was out late at night and sleeping at odd hours and in odd places; in fact, Cuthbert had caught the crow eating his hat while it was still on his head as he slept balanced on the stile.

As Cuthbert batted the crow away, Percy awoke just in time to see his assailant with his hand raised. This resulted in Percy over-balancing, his wellies flying upwards and Cuthbert being watched with suspicion for days.

At that moment, Percy was crawling through the undergrowth trying to see what Geraldine was doing as she pushed further into the older part of the Valley.

Geraldine was an Archaeologist and the local museum curator, but she usually restricted herself to scouring old displays in the museum store rooms. These recent field trips were most unusual and Percy thrived on the unusual; he adjusted the bracken stuck into his hat and moved slowly forward.

A member of the Valley mafia kicked his companion and with complicated signals announced that 'The twerp is moving forward following the nut-job from the museum.'

Being half asleep at the time, his fellow tracker misinterpreted this as 'Let's go home, the Mars bars are on me'.

The first member was then trampled by the second member as apparently hunger is the better part of valour.

Percy looked around at the sudden scuffle behind him, but the grass was closing over the recent activity and he shrugged, but as he returned his gaze to Geraldine, there was no sign of her. Percy increased the speed of his panther crawl until the ground fell away beneath him.

* * *

Ronald meanwhile sat high in a tree observing all these pathetic attempts at guile and concealment; he shook his head ruefully.

If these clowns had been in as many conflicts as he had, they would know that all that crawling only gives you sore knees and bracken-rash.

No, the seasoned mercenary would get there early and find a high vantage point where he could see everything and no-one could sneak up on him.

He had watched Geraldine duck into a cave when the mafia had unexpectedly broken cover.

5

Percy had also entered a cave, but from above and at twice the speed he had expected.

Ronald stretched his arms and prepared to climb down now that he spotted the area of activity. 'Amateurs,' he thought as he began to climb down and the rope tied by the mafia tightened around his leg. With a strangled cry, Ronald jerked sideways as one leg unexpectedly shot upwards and everything else pointed down. This left him swinging gently upside down from a tree like the pendulum from a Black Forest cuckoo clock.

The remaining mafia operative glanced at his watch and shook his wrist causing the big hand to fall from Mickey Mouse and leaving him none the wiser as to tea-time. He sighed and started to crawl backwards clamping his lips together to resist calling out "Cuckoo" to Ronald.

* * *

Geraldine stood in the dark listening intently, something was moving towards her in the cave. They were not ordinary footsteps, they made a dragging sound with a slight 'Flip-flop' back beat. Geraldine tightened her grip on the specimen hammer she carried for fossil hunting, whilst the voices in her head kept her company and provided encouragement. On their command, she swung the hammer, felt the impact and fled.

Chapter Two

If Cuthbert had been graced with normal reactions, he would have jumped when Percy kicked open the door, but as it was, he studied his friend and noted the bracken in his hat, the mud on his knees and wellies and the fact that Percy's hat seemed to be riding high as if there was something under it.

"Had a nice day?" he tried innocently, Percy glared.

* * *

In the Mandrake Arms later that evening, the atmosphere was quite subdued. Ronald was limping, Percy had an ice-pack on his head and then his hat on top of that and Geraldine sat in a corner with a hammer in her hand.

Ronald's brother Henry had been a news reporter reporting from frontlines which he had never visited and he began to try his hand at teasing out the facts as his wife Marjorie cleaned a glass so she could stay in one spot and watch.

"Nasty bump you've got there Percy," he tried.

Percy glared.

Henry tried Ronald, "Nasty limp you've got there Ronald."

Ronald glared.

Henry sighed and turned his charm on Geraldine, "Nasty hammer you've got there Geraldine, not sure we allow offensive weapons in here."

Geraldine glared, "You want it?" she hissed menacingly.

Henry joined his wife trying to make glass even more transparent than it already was.

Marjorie banged the glass down sharply causing everyone except Cuthbert to jump and even he thought about it. "What's going on?" she demanded, "If we wanted to be this miserable we would go to Cuthbert's and analyse his tea."

Cuthbert thought about this. On the one hand it was flattering that his kitchen would be chosen, but on the other hand he was rather proud of his unique beverages, especially when the milk was suspect and he added embalming fluid.

"Well!" demanded Marjorie staring at each of them in turn.

Her husband quailed, "I wasn't even there" he spluttered.

"Where?" demanded Marjorie.

Henry tugged at his collar and gasped, "Wherever they were."

Ronald nodded and adjusted his sore leg; Percy nodded and winced as the lump on his head throbbed, whilst Geraldine tapped the hammer against her palm.

Marjorie suddenly seemed distracted as if someone had tugged at her apron. Her hand went below the bar level and came back with a scruffy piece of paper. "Them woz," she began before correcting herself, "They were up the old end of the Valley." Marjorie's voice turned to silk, "Alright boys and girls; why were you at the old end of the Valley and why are you all injured?"

"I'm not!" spat Geraldine.

Marjorie never started a nut-cutlet by breaking the hardest nut, so her gaze swung to Percy, "What were you doing up there dear?"

Percy's eyes flickered around the room desperately because when Marjorie said 'dear' she meant expensive as in the Valley mafia charging for transport to A&E and very suspect blood transfusions.

"Gardening!" he spluttered immediately, assuming his default mode.

Marjorie came out from behind the bar and sidled around the tables until she was behind Percy.

"Good soil out there is it Percy?" she asked whipping off his ice pack and causing his hat to spin, before settling back on the only home that would have it.

Marjorie gasped. The wound on Percy's head seemed familiar; she'd seen that shape before.

Turning slowly towards the sound of Geraldine still tapping the hammer into her palm, Marjorie placed a lot of the pieces of the puzzle together immediately, even if the protagonists hadn't.

Ronald wiped the smirk off his face as he sensed Marjorie behind him, but he wasn't unduly worried as he had laid in ambush for the best of them and fought off far greater odds than this.

The sight of a member of the Valley mafia suddenly scuttling away under the tables should have rung alarm bells, but it didn't, so Ronald rose to meet the challenge, or he tried to. Suddenly, finding himself tied to the chair as he stood to face Marjorie, he tumbled backwards and lay with his feet in the air like a stranded tortoise.

"Tick-tock," mocked a small voice from under a nearby table.

Ronald now knew that he had been seen swinging from the tree and he also had a suspicion about who had cut him down and left him to roll downhill for what seemed an eternity.

As Marjorie looked from one to the other, Cuthbert decided upon a tactic to do something noble and back his friend Percy up, but before he could open his mouth, Percy out-thought him and said "It was Cuthbert, he made me do it!"

Marjorie's eyes swept across to Cuthbert as she thought, 'The plot thickens and so do the culprits.' With a disarming smile, Marjorie tried to read something in Cuthbert's carefully neutral expression.

Cuthbert didn't know that it was careful or neutral; his facial muscles simply rearranged themselves into a non-threatening passive stance until the threat went away.

"Well?" prompted Marjorie, raising one eyebrow like an invitation to enter the gates of hell.

"Well," Cuthbert began, thinking faster than his feet had ever moved. "The last I saw of either Percy or Ronald was when they were trying on frocks from the theatre company's store."

The atmosphere became static; breathing ceased and even Geraldine forgot to tap her hammer.

Percy jumped to his feet to rebut the allegations in his best courtroom manner, but stopped as the pain caught up with the movement and sat heavily with his head in his hands.

Ronald meanwhile wriggled furiously on his back like a fly stuck to a roll of sticky tape.

Margery accepted another piece of screwed up paper from beneath a table and frowned as she deciphered it. "So, basically Geraldine went for a walk carrying a hammer, Percy just happened to be gardening in the vicinity and fell down a hole near to where Ronald was bungee-jumping from a tree in the middle of nowhere and Cuthbert saw their ghosts trying on frocks in Marks and Spectres, is that it?"

All around her, heads nodded at this version of events, because the variables were too terrible to contemplate.

Marjorie returned to behind the bar and poured herself a large clear liquid before handing an orange juice to a scruffy hand which promptly whisked it away.

"Time gentlemen please," sighed Marjorie in resignation.

Chapter Three

The atmosphere around Cuthbert's table was wary to say the least. Ronald had been glaring at Cuthbert for some time, before he muttered "Frocks, trying on frocks?"

Cuthbert didn't have many spontaneous moments and he had been quite proud of that one, but there was something in Ronald's tone which consolidated all the neutral molecules in his face as Ronald continued.

"Do you remember when we didn't get on too well Cuthbert?" he asked.

Images of flying daggers and mysterious events flashed through Cuthbert's mental incident log and he nodded slowly as he rose to make the tea.

Everyone else seemed preoccupied. Percy was rubbing some homemade concoction on the bump on his head and flies were dropping dead on his shoulders.

Henry had spotted Marjorie gathering the Valley mafia which was never a good sign and the Captain was arranging a line of ants into an approximation of the battle of Austerlitz. He had just picked up a splinter from Cuthbert's ancient oak table whilst herding his cavalry ants into line and he was muttering about Cuthbert's furniture being so old that the Queen Anne legs all had varicose veins.

Cuthbert was gently stirring something odd into Ronald's tea when he sensed movement behind him; it was the type of noise someone sneaking up might make if they had fallen out of a tree and developed a limp.

Ronald was holding an Italian stiletto, the favoured knife of assassins everywhere and he held it at shoulder height as Cuthbert turned to present him with his piping hot mug of tea, 'accidentally' jerking it upwards.

"Do you know what this is Cuth?..., aaaargh!" shrieked Ronald.

"Blood?" asked Cuthbert dispassionately as he noted that Ronald's attempt to protect his eyes had sliced off his own left eyebrow.

The Captain exclaimed, "Good Lord Cuthbert, whoever trained you really knew his stuff; Ronald is a professional and you best him every time," as his ants beat a retreat in the confusion.

Ronald was stumbling about bumping into things as the mystery ingredient in his tea glued his eye lashes together and the stiletto waved about slicing and dicing the dead flies on Percy's shoulders.

Henry reached up and pulled his brother into a chair with a sigh. For a successful mercenary and a deadly assassin, he certainly took some nurse-maiding.

Percy looked up and noticed Ronald's missing eyebrow, shuffled to get comfortable and said, "One of my ancestors did research at a famous university on the purpose of eyebrows you know."

"Oh yes, which one?" Henry asked.

Percy scratched his bump gingerly, "both of them."

Henry furrowed his eyebrows, "both of which?" he asked, already dreading the answer.

"Both eyebrows," stated Percy with a shrug before thinking it through and adding, "Tobias Plumm I think, why?"

Henry sighed, "Not which Plumm, which university?"

"Does it matter?" asked Percy suspiciously.

"It might do," said Henry "Some universities are more eyebrow than others."

Percy watched Henry very carefully before continuing, "One theory was that they could be used to semaphore messages if you were a hostage and the bad guys had tied you up."

"How long ago was this?" asked the Captain.

"Why?" asked Percy.

"Well," continued the Captain, "If it was before money was invented what would the ransom be?"

"Beads?" suggested Henry.

"Cows?" tried Cuthbert.

"Pickled ancestor of Cuthbert," growled Ronald as the mystery ingredient began to affect his jaw.

"I don't know!" spluttered Percy, "It doesn't matter what the ransom was; the point is that they could signal somebody."

Cuthbert was getting into this now and he contributed, "She couldn't signal if she was a hairless."

"A hairless?" echoed the group around the table.

11

"Yes," said Cuthbert getting excited. "They would kidnap a hairless because she was coming into money and she couldn't signal anyone because she didn't have eyebrows." He sat back content that his point had been made.

After a brief silence, Henry asked quietly, "Cuthbert, do you mean an heiress?"

The silence stretched to the point where no one could remember what the last noise was and when they paid attention, again Percy had given up and gone.

Chapter Four

Avril sat at her desk with her back to the big window overlooking the street. She wasn't tempted to turn and stare through it because at the front of her desk was Geraldine and no one turned their backs on Geraldine if they could help it.

At that moment, Geraldine was deep in thought and chewing the end of a pencil. Several other chewed remnants of pencils lay around on Avril's office floor which was causing some distress to the reporter for the Triple Echo. When she had first started the job in this backwater, the editor had assured her that it was a stepping stone to a city job, but if this was a stepping stone, she couldn't see the other bank of the river from here. In fact, if she couldn't put an end to these liquid similes, it would be her watery grave.

Her other concern was her Editor's original promise, "Every time you send me a scoop, I'll buy you a new pencil," but so far Avril had bought all her own pencils and she was being forced to watch Geraldine savouring every one of them.

It wasn't as if nothing happened in the Valley, it was just that the Valley was very discreet about it.

She had tried interviewing Cuthbert for gossip, but he had an obsession with the spiral on her notebook and it was most disconcerting watching his eyes swivel as he tried to follow its route.

The Valley mafia had resisted all attempts at bribery, because whenever she was out negotiating with one of them, the others were opening her safe and rifling through the jelly-babies, lollipops and other treats which they regarded as currency and Avril was left with no leverage at all.

"This is the big one," exclaimed Geraldine suddenly.

Avril stared at the pencil noting that it had started out exactly the same as the others and was now reduced to a soggy little stub just like the rest of them. "Err, how is that one the big one?" she asked.

"Not the pencil," snapped Geraldine. "Weren't you listening?"

"You've sat there for hours and never said a thing," wailed Avril in desperation.

Geraldine looked at the reporter thoughtfully and said, "Well I've been waiting for you to interview me, never mind now, what do you think?"

"Think about what?" Avril could sense her sanity and her career racing away together into the sunset.

"The dinosaurs of course; please pay attention woman, this could be big news."

Geraldine was leaning forward intently now and watching Avril as if one of her fossils had moved.

Avril let out a breath, she had no idea where Geraldine was going with this but seeing as she was the museum curator and local archaeologist, she deserved a hearing.

"I can't help thinking that a headline consisting of 'The Dinosaurs are Dead,' will ever shake the world somehow," ventured Avril. "What do you expect, the world sealed off with crime-scene tape and policemen doing a fingertip search of every continent?"

Geraldine's riposte was simple, "No, just the Valley."

Avril gaped, "The Valley" she spluttered, "Why the Valley?"

Geraldine tipped her head to one side as if it made her voice penetrate a simple mind much quicker and said, "Because that's where I found the footprint."

Avril turned her chair through three hundred and sixty degrees until she faced Geraldine again, somehow it seemed to line her thoughts up. "But," she protested, "That sounds like something from that old film, The Land that Time Forgot."

Geraldine took the last pencil and tucked it behind her ear for later and stood to leave; she turned as she reached the door and said "Well, doesn't that sum this place up?"

Avril sat alone in her office and whispered, "The Valley That Time Forgot" and then began to scrabble on the floor for a useable pencil stub.

Chapter Five

One of the Valley mafia was scuttling along behind a low stone wall with a stuffed duck strapped to his head as a disguise, he was keeping pace with Henry and Ronald as they left Cuthbert's and he listened intently.

The contents of Cuthbert's tea were wearing off and Ronald had regained his speech and he was berating his brother for never backing him up.

Henry stopped and looked his brother in the eye or where he thought his eye would be, because it was getting dark. "Look Ronald, everyone has settled down in this Valley, so why not accept that however unlikely it might seem. Cuthbert is better trained than you and he's on some sort of witness protection programme."

Ronald was affronted.   In his time, he had removed world leaders and toppled countries. Occasionally, it had been deliberate too; no-one could convince him that he had lost his edge. He stopped and swivelled suddenly, his arm a blur. The knife flashed in the last of the suns rays and then flashed again as it came back at him.

Henry and Ronald dived to the ground with Henry shouting "What on earth are you doing?" through a mouthful of soil.

Ronald was getting up and pointing soundlessly at a bare wall "That duck!" he whispered, "It threw my knife back."

* * *

Percy had set off early to retrace his steps to the cave without knowing that Ronald was behind him at a discreet distance dressed in his tactical multi-pocketed all-terrain suit. The people at the snipers' academy had assured him that if he 'went static,' or the modern term 'went dark,' he would be invisible. He had spent a lot of forged money and dedicated a lot of other people's time to perfecting this look, whereas the mafia chap behind him merely had a stuffed duck on his head.

Percy licked his thumb and turned it this way and that gauging the wind. Then he paced out the distance between himself and a very tall tree and triangulated the height to use in his calculations. Next, he

15

stepped sideways to avoid some nettles and fell straight down the hole he was looking for.

Ronald was suddenly alert, the twerp had disappeared or was it a ruse and he was back-tracking to confuse any pursuer. It had worked, Ronald was confused.

The Valley mafia operative on active duty this morning shook his head and the stuffed duck feebly wobbled its own in sympathy.

He watched Ronald dash from tree to tree before tripping and falling headlong into a patch of nettles before he rolled over and over, scratching furiously as he fell into a hole.

The mafia tracker sighed and ambled over to the site of the disappearing adults; he had begun to wish that he'd been taking notes.

Percy was marching further and further into the cave, with only the slap-slap of his turned down wellies to keep him company, his gardeners second sight helped him to instinctively avoid obstacles except for roots, rocks and unidentified squishy things which ran off squeaking. He stopped to listen and then turned to face the way he had come. There was a series of strange lights coming towards him accompanied by an unearthly scratching sound. Percy squeezed himself into a shallow depression in the side wall and waited until the apparition was level with him, "Boo!" he shouted.

Ronald jumped in alarm and began to punch and kick at a tangle of roots until a familiar snigger caused him to turn.

Percy picked up one of the tactical lights which had fallen from Ronald's high-tech suit and clipped it onto his hat, "Watch-a doing Ronald?" he asked watching the other man scratch furiously. "Nice outfit" he added "Is it new?"

Ronald glared at him with all the force of all the tactical lights still fastened to him and snarled, "Best in the business, tear-proof, scratch-proof, water-proof and gas-proof."

"Not nettle–proof though eh?" asked Percy watching him scratch.

* * *

Cuthbert was having one of those peaceful interludes when the world actually seemed to have forgotten about him. He was at peace and he was a man without boundaries, mostly because his fences had fallen down. He knew it wouldn't last, but he basked in the moment and strolled across his farmyard at one with himself and with his animals. Or he would have been if he could find any of them.

* * *

Ronald and Percy begrudgingly strolled through the cave together, Ronald had to think of something to say before Percy embarked on some tale about his ancestors teaching pigeons to talk so they could deliver messages or something else equally outlandish. "So, is this one of the tunnels or something else?" he tried.

Percy was strangely quiet and preoccupied "Err, it's a cave, I think" he replied.

Ronald stopped and turned to face him, "Alright, what's the matter with you?

Percy hesitated, shuffled and eventually pointed at the cave floor and whispered, "I'm just not looking forward to meeting whatever left these footprints."

Ronald looked down and sure enough, there were three-toed footprints leading away into the darkness; there was something odd about these and Ronald dropped to one knee as all the best trackers do in the movies. "These are embedded in the stone," he said in awe, "They must be thousands of years old from before the rocks were hard." He began to scratch again.

"Jurassic?" asked Percy.

"No, just those damned nettles," said Ronald absently.

They followed the prints further and further into the cave and Ronald gave Percy tips on how to follow the spoor of a creature.

Percy couldn't help but think that it was relatively easy as this one had been dead for thousands of years and wasn't going to suddenly nip off in a different direction when it heard them coming, but he kept quiet, even Percy realised that being in a cave with Ronald wasn't the best situation he could imagine.

Ronald shone a light across the footprint at an oblique angle and exclaimed, "Look, it was injured, one footstep is deeper than the other; it was limping."

Percy was impressed, "How do you know all this stuff?" he asked.

Ronald straightened up scratched and stretched his back before replying, "I had a native tracker once, fantastic he was, taught me all he knew."

"What happened to him?" asked Percy wide eyed.

"I lost him."

The cave suddenly seemed very silent and very deep.

* * *

The crow watched Cuthbert hunting for his animals and shook his head. He'd seen this dolt lose dead bodies, so to have him missing live animals was no surprise to anyone.

Of course, the crow eating the chicken feed had convinced them to look for pastures new, or it had when he had led the fox in their direction.

Bulls were a sore point with Cuthbert, the horns made a point and Cuthbert ended up sore.

In fact from the crow's vantage point the only creatures left seemed to be the mice in the thatched roof.

* * *

Ronald and Percy sat on a rock outside the cave and waited for their breathing to return to normal. Nobody had given the order to panic and run, it just seemed the right thing to do at the time.

Ronald's nettle-rash seemed to have settled, so he began to rummage through his survival pockets, bringing out high energy bars and a tube connected to a re-hydration sack called a camel-bak, hidden on his back.

Percy snorted with derision and dug into his welly, bringing out a soggy digestive biscuit which promptly folded in half around his fingers. Looking at Ronald he asked hopefully, "Swap?"

Chapter Six

Geraldine was deep in the vaults of the museum, she would have to really research her subject because she hadn't studied dinosaurs or their footprints. In fact, her dissertation had been deliberately obscure, something about Sumerian writing instruments designed for left-handed midgets if she remembered correctly. It had certainly worked; no last minute appearance of some expert on the subject to refute her analysis and deny her the diploma, but she'd printed out a fake just in case.

* * *

Cuthbert's table once again became the scene for a council of war. When all the tea-stirring and clanking, coughing and shuffling had run its course, the Captain and Henry exchanged glances and the Captain looked around the table.

Cuthbert sat at the head where he could dash to the temperamental cooking range should it suddenly decide to erupt and cover everyone in ash.

Ronald and Percy sat side-by-side on one side like conspirators facing the Captain and Henry on the other.

The Captain exercised his eye for detail and noted that Ronald was wearing a camouflaged suit with empty power-bar wrappers sticking out of one of the many pockets. He also had a stray tube hanging over one shoulder, a pressure mark around his forehead where a head torch had been and he was scratching. All this caused him to conclude that Ronald had been somewhere dark and private where he could practice the bagpipes when he had been set upon by a creature and had to feed it power-bars whilst he escaped through poison ivy.

This would explain the scream and the new friendship with Percy could indicate a heroic rescue by the odd little twerp. Putting all this together, he nodded towards Percy and said, "Well done that man, heroic effort" and to Ronald, "Nothing to be ashamed of you know, we all have our vices."

Percy would take praise from anywhere, so he beamed and sat back contentedly.

Ronald however glared at the Captain, "The only vice I've got is the one I use for interrogations and it's firmly bolted down mate."

The Captain gulped.

Henry looked around and sighed, "Well, why are we here, does anyone know about the scream?"

Percy sat up, "Oh yes! That was a family tragedy that was."

Everyone began to mentally tackle the demons conjured up by the thoughts of Percy's family moving into the Valley, the tragedy wouldn't be *theirs*.

Percy continued, "One of my ancestors was an artist, he was a great one for painting emotions, he painted some woman with an enigmatic smile, a depressed boy in a silk suit and a chap screaming." He had an exhibition in a café owned by a chap named Mustafa Munch and the next thing he knew was it was being called Munch's Scream and it was famous."

Ronald patted Percy's arm, "Do you want to borrow my vice mate? We'll go and find him and make munch-meat out of him."

Percy paused and actually looked as if he was considering Ronald's offer, but then he carried on. "My first job was following the family tradition of being an artist you know." He gazed wistfully around the table as the rest of them gazed wistfully at the exit.

"I had just completed a magnificent piece of pavement art when the police came along and said "Nothing fancy mate, just a chalk outline where the body was will do."

Henry looked on in astonishment as all normal boundaries of sanity were scattered by the winds of Percy's imagination and rendered redundant.

"Why are we here?" he repeated and rapped the table whose ancient timbers were offended and rapped him back causing him to suck his knuckles.

"The footprints" said Ronald as if no-one had been paying attention.

"Footprints?" echoed Henry and the Captain, "What footprints?"

Percy took over and began speaking in awed tones, "Secret footprints, thousands of years old, never before seen by human eyes."

"Oh, *those* footprints" said Cuthbert.

"You knew?" spluttered Percy.

"Of course, we played in them as children jumping from one foot to the other to see who could go the furthest."

"Who did?" asked the Captain.

"Me," replied Cuthbert wistfully, they didn't tell me about the crevasse and I travelled as far down as I had done across."

It was quiet around the table as some of them wondered how Cuthbert had survived and Ronald wondered *why* he had.

Chapter Seven

Geraldine was holding forth in the Mandrake Arms and lecturing the other women upon the rise of the dinosaurs and how the Valley itself had barely changed over time. Geraldine, being the museum curator held several certificates with mock fancy red seals on the bottom and they were framed on the wall of her office.

Avril, the local reporter for the Triple Echo newspaper only had a swimming certificate on her wall, so of course she deferred to Geraldine.

Elspeth, the Captain's wife was an enigma. She had travelled all over the world with her husband and some of the things she had done were never admitted to either officially or privately, mostly to avoid ruinous compensation payments by her Majesties government.

The only things on Marjorie's office wall were crayon drawings of stick figures which represented wanted posters issued by the Valley mafia which was still very much under her control.

Geraldine was demonstrating the different roaring and rumblings of the dinosaurs to demonstrate what a wild place the Valley must have been when Elspeth asked "Did these dinosaurs have ears then dear?"

Geraldine stopped in mid-flow and her all encompassing vocabulary was reduced to "Pardon?"

"Well" continued Elspeth, "The Captain and I have been in museums all over the world and none of the dinosaurs seem to have ears."

"Well they wouldn't would they?" spluttered Geraldine, they're mostly bones or fossils now aren't they?" Even as her superior knowledge and education dripped from her words, a tiny alarm bell was ringing as she realised that this was Elspeth she was dealing with.

Marjorie came around the bar and made herself comfortable and Avril eased her notebook onto her lap, let the games begin.

Elspeth took a breath and began, "Well dear, as fascinated as I was by your demonstration of the dinosaurs alarm calls, I just wondered why they bothered if the other dinosaurs couldn't hear them, because they didn't have ears."

Geraldine gaped, this was like being confronted by Percy; surely one of Elspeth's ancestors hadn't been a cavewoman, but then panic chased confusion across the back of her eyes as she accepted that all of them had cavewomen as ancestors.

Geraldine began to shuffle imaginary papers into neat piles in front of her and then suddenly bade her companions goodnight and left.

"Oh dear," said Elspeth, "I hope I didn't ruin a fascinating discourse for you both" glancing at Marjorie and Avril in turn. "Not at all," smiled Marjorie, "Another sherry dear?"

Chapter Seven

Around Cuthbert's table, the talk was centred upon war. The Captain and Ronald were recreating the battle of somewhere or other and demonstrating the tactics with mugs spoons and pepper pots, whilst Cuthbert idly stared at a crack in his ceiling and wondered which side of the house he would live in if it fell in half.

Percy seemed distracted by something in one of his wellies and Henry interrupted with a thought of his own.

"You know," he began, "I have a theory that the root of all war is punctuation."

Ronald and the Captain took it in turns with, "Eh?" and "Is that some kind of weapon?"

Henry waved a hand to still any more rampant speculation and said, "No, you clots, punctuation. I'm convinced that if the comma had been outlawed, the war would have ended far sooner."

"How on earth would that work?" spluttered the Captain

Henry smiled, "Well, without all those commas, it would have reached a full stop much quicker."

Percy scoffed at them all, "you think *you've* been under pressure? I worked on a toy production line making figures of Dracula; there were only two of us, so I made every second count."

The Captain and Ronald simply carried on where they had left off, Percy began poking a wooden spoon into his welly and Cuthbert had decided to live in the side with the door, otherwise it would be draughty if he couldn't close it.

Henry sighed.

* * *

The next morning Percy came down in a panic; his wellies were on the wrong feet and he kept colliding with things, probably because his hat was on backwards.

Cuthbert took a breath before asking, "What's wrong Percy?"

Percy gave him a panic-stricken look, "I've woken up in a time-warp" he said "The sun is high, but my clock says 8.00 am, I'm late."

24

A puzzled Cuthbert asked "Late for what? You never go anywhere, and anyway, did you only look at one clock?"

Percy snorted, "Why do I need more than one clock? Both eyes point in the same direction."

Cuthbert thought for a moment before asking, "Is that the clock you bought from the Valley mafia yesterday?"

"Yes," replied Percy "It's really quiet, not like that clonking old thing," sneering in the direction of Cuthbert's long-case clock which promptly skipped a beat in shock.

Cuthbert narrowed his eyes and asked, "You mean that clonking old thing which says 11.55 am and matches the position of the sun outside?"

Percy hesitated, "Maybe," sensing his grip loosening on the situation.

For once Cuthbert was relentless, "You do realise that the Valley mafia only own one battery and they always take it back out when they sell anything?"

Percy eyed him suspiciously, but he knew from bitter experience that Cuthbert's expressions were unreadable, so he stomped off imagining all the things he would have done to the mafia if he hadn't been terrified of them.

Cuthbert stroked the antique oak casing of the clock and it gave an appreciative 'ding' in return.

Chapter Eight

Geraldine was getting tired, the museum's basement was a treasure trove if your idea of treasure was mould, dust, cardboard and mouse droppings. She sighed as yet another cardboard file fell apart in her hands and added to the powdery carpet building up on the floor. She soon wouldn't be able to see her footprints from earlier and retrace her steps. The thought of being trapped in here with a load of mice who only seemed to nibble the bottom of everything caused her to grab one last file and take it to her office; that way, it wasn't far to the bins if it turned out to be another study of a Valley with strange inhabitants which ended with an ink blot and the squiggle of a broken nib as if the writer had left in a hurry.

* * *

The Mandrake Arms seemed to give off a contented hum of atmosphere as seats were scraped and drinks were placed. It was like the opera where everyone waited for the hubbub to die down and the coughing to stop.

Henry, the Captain, Ronald, Cuthbert and Percy were all in attendance which was as it should be for a secret meeting

Henry briefly reminded them all that he had been a successful journalist, before Ronald reminded Henry that he had only been successful thanks to him, and the Captain reminded them that if they had seen half the things he had seen, they would be *really* successful.

"The point is," snapped Henry trying to assert authority over two 'Know-it-alls',' one psychopathic fantasist and Cuthbert. "I have the contacts to make the most of this story when the bodies start to appear."

This got Cuthbert's attention immediately, "Not again, I've hardly buried anyone lately and none of the alarms have gone off."

"Alarms?" queried Henry, "How does that work?"

Ronald sniggered, "He stacks empty glass jam-jars on top of the graves so that if anyone digs their way out, the jars fall with a clatter."

"And do they?" asked the Captain.

26

"Do they do what?" asked Ronald absently, as his senses alerted him to an intruder.

"Clatter," persisted the Captain.

"Not since we sold them to the woman in sandals in the next Valley to put scented candles in." said Jasper.

"How did you get in here?" demanded Henry, turning to confront the leader of the Valley mafia.

"It's a pub isn't it?" came the reply.

After a quick glance around, everyone replied "Yes."

"Well, pub's have doors don't they?"

This was Henry's domain and he rose to the bait, "Yes, and this is my pub and there is a sign over the door saying, no-one under eighteen allowed to enter."

Jasper cocked his head to one side and said, "Now, what sort of idiot would put a sign up that high so that people under eighteen couldn't read it?"

Henry spluttered and looked around for inspiration; he came up with, "This is a secret meeting."

"Oh," said Jasper "Pay attention lads, this is a *secret* meeting."

Shadows detached themselves from all sides and dark corners as the Valley mafia convened a meeting within a meeting.

"Any other business?" asked Jasper. "I believe that bodies have been mentioned."

Chapter Nine

The ladies sat around Elspeth's kitchen table and waited until she had fussed and dusted and generally re-arranged things, until they were back exactly where they had started.

Geraldine was a source of great distress to Elspeth at the moment, there seemed to be dust dropping from her every time she moved.

Marjorie looked fondly at her companions; Avril the local reporter had her notebook open and ready, even though the Valley had sucked every scrap of enthusiasm out of here.

Arkle had returned from one of her trips where she took part in breaking horses. When you looked at the size of her, you simply had to feel sorry for the horse. At that moment, she was trying to perch on a chair with the expression of someone who didn't know whether to saddle it or put it out of its misery.

Geraldine shuffled some dry papers and dust motes floated upwards, causing Elspeth to dash for emergency cleaning accessories.

Marjorie waited for calm to be restored before asking, "Right girls, what do we do about this new obsession the men have got hold of. Will it affect the status quo?"

Avril scribbled furiously until Marjorie laid a hand over hers and said, "No dear, the rock band won't be coming to the Valley."

* * *

Ronald watched the proceedings very carefully and slowly slid his hand down towards the knife he kept in his boot, only to find that the mafia already had it.

That kid across the table was cleaning his fingernails with it.

Ronald would recognise him again, because he was wearing a Mickey Mouse watch with only one finger. The odd thing was that he wore it hanging down from his lapel instead of around his wrist.

Ronald gritted his teeth and never noticed that all his other possessions and accessories had been redistributed.

Chapter Ten

Martin Hepplewhite had been antique dealing in the next Valley all his life and his skills at distressing wood, marble and metals meant that he was older than most of his so-called antiques.

He was just smearing a reproduction statue with yoghurt and bird droppings in his courtyard at the back when his shop bell clanged; wiping his hands and adjusting his smile, he dashed into his shop hoping for a coach load of gullible tourists, but was faced with an empty shop.

Martin started to shake; he'd been here before when those awful twins from the next Valley had been trying to sell him anything that wasn't nailed down.

Stepping forward and leaning over his counter like a man peering over a precipice, he gasped.

Looking back at him were two not very clean faces and one seemed to be wearing a Mickey Mouse watch upside down on his lapel.

Before Martin could clear his throat and ask anything, a voice came from his left, "You was recommended to us mister" it said.

Martin gulped and turned to see Jasper standing by a display of Japanese weapons and sliding a fake samurai sword from its sheath.

"Be careful," he spluttered, "That's sharp."

Jasper took out a pocket-knife, unfolded it, sliced a sliver of mahogany from Martin's display counter and replied "Nah! *that's* sharp."

Martin's face was changing colour "You're the mafia aren't you, those twins from the next Valley sent you didn't they?"

Jasper jammed the Japanese sword into the wooden floor and leant his weight on it to make it bend in a very un-samurai way.

"The twins have, how shall we put this, moved on?" he said, releasing the sword so that it 'boinged' from side to side. "I'm the head of the Valley mafia now and we might be bringing some business your way."

Martin studied the three scruffs before him; they didn't have the same air of menace as the twins, perhaps he could indeed do business with them.

Martin tried levity, "So, under new management eh? Perhaps you're not as rigid as the last lot and I can put some pocket money your way eh lads?"

Jasper studied him before asking, "Ever heard of the iron hand in the velvet glove?"

Martin ignored any sense of dread and quipped, "Velvet glove eh, is it for sale, be worth more as a pair you know."

The silence dragged on punctuated by the decreasing 'boing' as the sword slowed in its tremors.

Martin failed to out-stare any of them and he tried for the, 'I've got the money' high ground. "I like the look of that Mickey Mouse watch you've got there son, parting with it are you?

The two in front of the counter gasped in unison and took a step back. Jasper sucked air in through his teeth. "Dangerous territory mate, dangerous territory."

Martin was annoyed, enough was enough. "Look, I can see it's damaged from here, it's got a finger missing, but it's a collectable and I can give you some sweetie money for it."

The air in the shop became frigid and time seemed to stand still (It actually did, because Martin never wound the clocks amongst his stock).

Jasper stepped closer and Martin took a matching step back as his potential assailant hissed, "That is no longer just a watch, it is a memento of a brave and honoured member of the Valley mafia who is no longer with us. It is worn with pride when awarded for outstanding deeds against mankind and is priceless to us".

This was a lot to take in; Martin wanted to correct Jasper and say don't you mean deeds for *the benefit* of mankind? But just in time, he remembered that this was the mafia and settled for "Why, where did he go? You said he was no longer with us."

Jasper studied him carefully and glanced at the other two members who were looking at the floor respectfully. "It belonged to our brave soldier Egbert, who has gone to live with his mother on a farm where he can romp in the fields and play with the animals all day."

Martin glanced at the kids in front of the counter who seemed to be wiping their eyes; he'd seen enough Disney films in his time to know what 'Gone to live on a farm' meant. "Sorry lads," he muttered.

30

This was actually true, Egbert really had gone to live with his mother on a farm, but the Valley mafia needed heroes just like anyone else.

With a wave of his hand, Jasper signalled for his 'men' to wait outside so that the business could begin. He started with, "There are strange creatures in the Valley and we can't put a price on them yet."

Martin stared as a kaleidoscope of visions rotated before him; Cuthbert, Percy, Ronald, Henry and of course that nice Marjorie.

He suddenly found that he was laughing hysterically and thumping his counter-top, "Oh, you've got strange creatures in the Valley all right my lad, they don't come any stranger and I defy anybody to put a price on them."

The doorbell clanged to signal Jasper's exit and Martin suddenly pulled himself together as he realised that the last words he heard had been, "I'll be back."

He gulped, he'd heard that somewhere before.

Chapter Eleven

Henry was alone in the Mandrake Arms. The rest of the men had automatically distanced themselves from the mafia and then the mafia had departed. Henry leaned back and closed his eyes to enjoy this moment of peace. It didn't last long, he could smell horse. Sitting up, Henry could see that he was surrounded, the women were staring at him intently and Margery was smiling, he gulped.

Now, Henry had seen the world, he had been a war reporter and a top journalist and he was credited with some mile-stone moments in reporting. It had been Henry who, when coming out of a nap and finding the film crew signalling furiously to him, had realised that he had forgotten to prepare his broadcast.

Arranging his face into a sombre reflection of the times, he had stared at the camera and intoned, "I am not at liberty to say where I've been or what I've seen, because the security of the nation depends upon my discretion. All I can say is that I counted all of our planes out and I counted all of them back in."

His female co-presenter gasped in surprise, "All of them?" she asked.

Henry paused, "Well, all the ones I saw anyway," he added.

His co-presenter wiped away a tear of patriotism and completely forgot that she and Henry had just opened the same Primary School just an hour ago and she hadn't seen a single aircraft. So Henry did not need to be reassured that he was quick thinking and he could cover his own back as well as any tortoise, but a circle of women? That was something else.

"A Café'?" spluttered Henry, who on earth would sit in a café'?"

"Tourists," explained Margery patiently.

"What tourists?" asked Henry, desperately looking around for reinforcements, but after seeing how close Arkle was sitting to the door, he slumped and tried to pay attention; the conversation span around him like a verbal kaleidoscope.

"Round tables," suggested Margery.

"Gingham table-cloths," suggested Avril

"With matching gingham curtains" added Elspeth.

"Menus with The Mandrake Arms Café heading," gasped Margery.

Henry sat up suddenly, "That's ridiculous; we can't have two Mandrake Arms."

The conversation stalled as the women paused for the slowest one to catch up and Margery could see that he had now, "Exactly dear, weren't you listening?"

Henry gasped in relief as Percy entered, but the gasp turned to distress as Arkle spun his potential ally around and ejected him.

Percy tried again and was ejected once more. This happened several times before Henry could grab him and pull him over to the bar, but by this time Percy had been spun so many times that his concentration was on 'cyclone' setting.

Henry whispered urgently to Percy, "They want to turn the Mandrake Arms into a tea-room or café or something, but it's a pub."

Margery snarled from behind the bar, "It's only a pub when it's full of loafers."

"Wouldn't that make it a shoe shop?" asked Percy trying to keep up.

Margery pressed ahead, "Full of loafers making a pint last all day and shuffling dominoes so that they rattle like skeletons dancing in a dustbin."

Henry tried to be conciliatory whilst Percy cleared his head and became of some use, so he hissed in the general direction of Percy's hat, "They want to make it a tea-room, not a pub."

Percy straightened; this was his territory "Mushroom eh? Good food that and a grub is protein, nice combination."

Henry hissed louder, "Tea-room, not mushroom you fool and pub not grub, and gingham Percy, gingham."

Percy tried to unlock his thoughts, but wherever he put his hand, he couldn't find a pint to lubricate things, so he sulked "bring 'em? Of course I didn't bring 'em, you never told me to bring 'em."

"Bring what?" asked Henry in desperation.

"The mushrooms and the other grub," said Percy making his way unsteadily to the door still sulking.

Cuthbert couldn't say that he was never taken by surprise, but he could definitely say that no-one else ever saw him taken by surprise, because the subtle shift in expression and the time delay involved in his reactions, pretty much cancelled each other out, but the hammering on his door when Percy was already inside was really straining his reputation.

Henry burst in gasping as if Arkle had mistaken him for Percy and remembered her last threat. He sat down heavily and watched as Cuthbert pushed a steaming cup in front of him, not having the strength to push it away; Henry watched the spoon slowly dissolve.

The Captain and Ronald had seen Henry sprinting for Cuthbert's farm so they changed direction, if it could make Henry break into a run, this would be momentous indeed and they had to be part of it.

When the Captain and Ronald sat at the table, Henry had recovered enough to gasp, "The women, they're making a café' in the valley."
No reaction.

"Here, in *this* valley" he tried, still nothing.

Henry took a deep breath and the words came out in a rush, "They're making a café in the Mandrake Arms and throwing out all the beer and covering everything in gingham."

The words were like a spluttering fuse of consciousness, the fire began to burn with the words Mandrake Arms, the flame began to race with the words throw out the beer, but the explosion was caused by the word gingham.

Every man has a trigger-point and to the majority of them that point is gingham, those pink and white squares of subtle femininity mocking the macho tones of a chess board. That innocence-invoking apron of kitchen culture acting as a screen for the diabolical concoctions prepared under its influence.

The men left Cuthbert's farm in an impassioned rage like torch-wielding villagers and set off to defend the Alamo or the Mandrake Arms, whichever they came across first because it was getting dark now.

Somehow, the main lounge in the pub already felt different, not just because the men sat inside a circle of women like a beleaguered wagon train, but all the talk of coffee and croissants seemed to have scoured the place of its atmosphere.

It had been explained painfully slowly to the men that this discovery of dinosaur footprints would bring attention to the valley and help to relieve some of the boredom.

34

When the men began to protest, the women had made it very clear that *they* were bored and the men were responsible. The plans were explained and everyone contributed their version of how the 'Theme Park/Nature Reserve/ mafia cash machine would work for everyone's benefit.

"Well?" asked Margery, making the word sound as if it had been sharpened and was now very dangerous indeed.

Henry adopted a nonchalant pose, which was somehow supposed to allay his comrades suspicions that he was weakening and at the same time show solidarity with his wife. He failed on both counts.

The Captain had huffed and puffed, but he knew how much Elspeth loved that damned gingham stuff and tomorrow was her day for home baking, so his mince pies were in jeopardy.

Ronald snorted his disdain and made to get up, but he paused at a growl from behind him. It was no big deal, he had wrestled grizzlies before, but when he realised that it was Arkle, he sat back down again.

Cuthbert had been quite worried until Margery had reassured him that the new café would not need to borrow his family recipe and that his last bit of instant coffee and sawdust would be safe.

Percy had been quietly taking it all in and reluctantly all eyes turned to him out of a politeness they would have preferred to ignore.

Margery raised her eyebrows in a semaphore warning recognised by everyone except Percy and asked, "Any questions Percy?"

Percy was looking down at his wellies as he swung his little legs under the table, but now he looked up brightly and asked, "Will it be a proper coffee café, with those proper café cups? And with those great big copper kettles, filling proper café cups, or will the public have to bring 'em, because of all that gingham, and so we won't have matching sets of all those proper coffee café cups?"

The silence was only broken by the gentle creaking of Percy's swinging wellies, which unfortunately for him reminded Margery of the creak of a corpse on a gibbet.

"Get him," she cried.

Chapter Twelve

Avril was pleased, at last she was in on the ground floor of a news story and she eyed the pristine sheet of paper in the typewriter before her, as if she was daring it to burst into flame in a last attempt to thwart her. Steep-ling her fingers to aid concentration, she allowed her chair to turn for one last gaze onto the street before she would cause the machine to clatter into life and lay the foundation for her future. Concentrating on a furtive movement in front of a row of shops, she leaned forward in her chair, what on earth was Percy up to? She wondered.

The Captain had been despatched for more baking supplies and as he stood in the queue at Mrs Biggle's, he added something macho to his wife's shopping list in case anyone saw him, what on earth is Percy up to? He also wondered.

Avril had given in to temptation and left her office with a notebook clutched firmly in her hand and a pencil behind her ear. She came face to face with the Captain about half-way along the street. They muttered "hello" and "how are you?" and realised that they had never actually held a conversation before.

The Captain waved a hand vaguely and muttered, "Just wondered where that chap Percy had gone."

Avril smiled, "me too, I saw him duck into this shop and I was intrigued."

The Captain scoffed, "It wasn't this shop my dear, it was the next one."

Avril double-checked before asserting, "No, he definitely went into this next one, I saw him."

The Captain shook his head ruefully, "My dear girl, I am a trained military observer and I saw where he went quite clearly."

Avril bristled at the dear girl label and replied, "And I am a trained journalist, I see the things others try to conceal."

"What do you mean?" asked the Captain suspiciously.

Avril looked him up and down and began rather slyly, "You *claim* to be a military man and yet you feel the need to disguise your wife's errands by placing something masculine on top of the eggs, butter and flour you have purchased."

The Captain spluttered *"claim, claim*? I was at the battle of where -is-it with what's-his-name, he can vouch for me and anyway, what about you?"

Avril stepped back, "What about me?" she hissed.

The Captain looked her up and down, "New notebook, blank pages and the price tag still dangling from it. The only thing you've used is the pencil behind your ear and that looks like a teething ring."

Avril snatched the chewed stub in question and was about to blame Geraldine when Percy stepped between them and with a breezy "Morning all," walked away before either of them could see where he had come from.

* * *

Geraldine had called a meeting, she had been rattled by having her expertise challenged by Elspeth and it was time to set the record straight and exert her authority at the same time.

The bar at the Mandrake Arms was full and most of the customers were gazing around wistfully. The men remembering where every beer-stain, knock, bump and scratch had come from to create this hallowed atmosphere and the women picturing, well basically, gingham.

Geraldine called the meeting to order and propped an illustrated chart on an easel where everyone could see it. "This," she began "Is a Brontosaurus, obvious because of its long neck making it instantly recognisable."

"Is that where bronchitis comes from when we have neck trouble?" asked Henry trying to be superior.

Geraldine glared "No, that sort of neck trouble comes from someone creeping up behind you and throwing a noose over a lamp-post."

Henry gulped.

Geraldine flipped another picture over on the chart of dinosaur types and tapped a pointer against a ferocious looking beast, "This is the Tyrannosaurus Rex," she announced.

"Hah" said Ronald, "That one died out because it couldn't open tins with its funny little front feet, so it starved."

Geraldine gaped as the laughter spread.

Percy contributed "He's the reason why dinosaurs stopped wearing clothes as well."

"Why?" asked the Captain with a giggle.

"Because Tyrannosaurus wrecks 'em" answered Percy.

Geraldine seethed as she turned another page to reveal a flightless bird-like creature. Raising her voice, she demanded attention and revealed that the modern thinking was that most of the dinosaurs didn't actually have scales, but in fact they had feathers.

The room fell silent as a memory percolated amongst the men.

Percy went quiet in the hope that all was forgotten, but the crow had been feeding on fallen crisps under the tables and Percy knew he was doomed, when the bird hopped onto the table, ruffled his head feathers, pointed at Percy and drew his wing across his own throat.

"That's right," exclaimed Henry, "The crow told us that 'the scruffy one had killed the great chicken."

Percy looked around in panic as everyone remembered him enclosing a giant chicken in pastry for a cooking competition and all the farmyard fowl reverently carrying it off for reburial in accordance with its legend.

"No I didn't, no I couldn't, no I wouldn't," spluttered Percy.

"Yes you did, yes you could and yes you would," chanted the men accompanied by a nodding crow.

The women looked on in awe as Marjorie asked, " So you lot found a giant chicken, Percy encased it in pastry and the farmyard chickens rescued it and reburied it and this might relate in some way to the footprints in the valley having feathers and being a race of giant chickens?"

The men nodded slowly, somehow things never sounded as clear-cut when Marjorie delivered *her* analysis.

Everyone decided to concentrate away in the opposite direction to Margery and they discovered that Geraldine had gone, leaving behind her easel and the picture with a very sharp pointer stabbed right through the forehead of a quite benign looking creature which now looked like a vicious Triceratops.

The meeting began to break up as Percy regaled them with a reference to his hunter-gatherer ancestor who was only frightened of one fearsome beast and that was the Doyouthinkisaurus?

Chapter Thirteen

Jasper had convened a meeting and he paced in front of his men. "There are plans a-foot gentlemen," he said, still pacing. "I've heard the women discussing a tearoom and the men blathering on about a theme park involving dinosaurs. It's all very ambitious for this dump, but where there's a will there's a way and where there's a profit, there's a mafia. Keep your ears open gentlemen, because never in the field of human incompetence has so much been achieved by so few, and that's before Percy joins in."

The men were sat around Cuthbert's table unaware that the last secret meeting where the plans were laid for a theme park had been overheard.

In fact, Jasper hadn't really needed to hide behind the plant this time, because he had stolen Henry's notes before he left the Mandrake Arms.

This resulted in a meeting/séance where vital pieces of paper and diagrams suddenly appeared on Cuthbert's table whilst Henry was still rummaging in his briefcase looking for them.

Jasper complicated things a bit because he was reading them in the wrong order before sliding them along the old table top causing Henry to announce that "some of the rides will be huge and we can even have animatronics," before he then announced that "a suitable site will be agreed by all."

"It sounds as if you've already made all the decisions yourself," humphed the Captain.

Ronald nodded in agreement and exchanged looks with the Captain. A share of the profits could be in jeopardy here and they shared a mutual concern.

Cuthbert and Percy only had one concern and they automatically sat closer together as another piece of paper materialised before them and the pot-plant rustled gently.

Percy whispered, "Did you see that?"

Cuthbert promptly shut his eyes and replied "I don't see anything, it's a law."

Every eye in the room widened at the sound of a prolonged whistle from behind the plant as Jasper read the last line on the last sheet of paper. "Have you seen the projected profits on this venture?" he hissed.

Henry stuck out his chest, "Oh yes sonny, I thought you'd be impressed, that will take some beating won't it?"

Jasper coughed, "Not really mate, I can double this *and* afford the animatronics and still pay you lot to dress up as clowns selling candy-floss at the entrance."

Jasper took the hint after the adults refused to discuss anything else in front of him and declared that he was going home to bed. Bending down to pick up his pot-plant, he stuck a listening device under a chair, just in case the one under the table failed.

Henry once again took control of the meeting "Right gentlemen, any questions?"

Percy raised his hand.

Henry sighed, "Any *real* questions? What about you Cuthbert?"

Cuthbert looked around in a panic and replied "Only the same one that he's got," indicating Percy.

"How do you know it's the same one?" asked Henry in disbelief.

Percy leant forward "Because it's the only sensible question which needs to be asked after all that information we've been given.

Henry waved his hand resignedly "All right, let's hear it."

Percy leaned back "Who is this Annie McTronic then and how much does *she* get out of it?"

Standing outside alone, Henry breathed in the cold night air and studied the stars above him. He knew that he had to go back in eventually, but he couldn't help but wonder what the odds were of him living here when there were all those uninhabited rocks out there in the silent vacuum of space where he could be at peace.

With a smile, he gave a shudder at the realisation that wherever he went, one of Percy's ancestors would have got there first.

He opened Cuthbert's door and re-entered the fray. There was a space at the table when Henry sat down and he was informed that after several explanations of animatronics being the mechanically powered animals they were hoping to use. Percy had made a bolt for the door (they all laughed at that as Percy was in charge of making things).

Chapter Fourteen

Margery was becoming annoyed. For an educated woman with a career, Avril could be really useless at times. She was a professional reporter for goodness sake and yet she couldn't find the shop Percy had come out of when she had stood right in front of him. They had walked down the street in one direction and then down in the other direction before splitting up and meeting in the middle, but there was nothing there that they hadn't seen before.

Avril was frustrated, but not frustrated enough to ask the Captain for help, because she suspected that these men were all in league with each other anyway.

Elspeth tried to be sympathetic and she offered, "Nobody gets everything right all the time dear; I failed my first driving test just after I had won my third race at Le-Mans."

This was a silent void crying out to be filled, so Margery asked cautiously "What happened?"

Elspeth allowed her shoulders to slump just to show that the emotions were still raw, before she replied "The examiner asked me what type of road sign I could expect to see on a country road and I answered 'pick your own strawberries."

Cuthbert had actually slept in; this was a rarity because farmers were usually slaves to their animals, but if they wandered off as many times as Cuthbert's used to, you became a slave to *looking* for the animals.

Cuthbert had experienced this once before when a fox had entered his chicken coop triggering his home-made alarm system which consisted of a trip-wire and his father's old blunderbuss.

Neither the fox nor the chickens came out of it well and Cuthbert found it easier to board the hen house door shut.

Anyway, as soon as Percy moved in there was no time for animals, it was like trying to herd rubber ducks up a waterfall just staying sane around him.

Cuthbert stopped dead as realisation struck him "Percy!" he hissed, that's what was missing; that's why he had overslept. There had been no noise of clanking frying pans, no exquisite smell of breakfast from Percy's fry-up, just before he cremated Cuthbert's portion.

There was something brewing, but it wasn't the tea because the kettle wasn't on.

Cuthbert wasn't alone for long, Henry and the Captain entered the kitchen and reached for the mugs of tea which simply weren't there.

Cuthbert sighed, never mind the plans for a café in the Valley, he already felt as if he ran one.

Henry indicated that four mugs were needed, so Cuthbert assumed that the mug outside was Ronald; it certainly fitted in with all the thuds and groans they could hear.

Eventually, curiosity about the noise defeated curiosity about the contents of the mugs and they all wandered outside; an interesting sight greeted them.

Ronald was on the floor on his back and Jasper was standing over him as the rest of the mafia looked on.

"Well done that man," enthused the Captain. "Teaching them how to fall eh?"

Ronald quickly scrambled to his feet and slipped a Swiss army knife into Jasper's hand to keep him quiet about what had really happened during the unarmed combat course and he started to limp towards the doorway. He never made it.

The air was suddenly sucked out of the farmyard and the ground began to shake. Cuthbert could recognise Percy's tractor anywhere, but the others were rooted to the spot as their survival instincts collided with the fight or flight signals and sheer panic over-ruled everything.

Cuthbert ground his teeth as his barn doors flew off their hinges yet again, but the grinding stopped for long enough to let his eyes goggle at the apparition advancing towards them. No-one should have panicked because the clues were all there, the clank of the caterpillar tracks, the horrendous noise, the belching smoke from the vertical exhaust and especially the fact that Percy was sat on top of the whole thing. But to counteract all these obvious signs, was the gigantic head swinging from side to side as this monstrosity lurched in their direction and the dust cloud raised by the dragging tail, not to mention the gentle clack of the razor sharp teeth every time the apparition hit a bump.

The mafia had disappeared over the stone wall as soon as they realised how much use a catapult would be against this thing.

The Captain had made a run for it under the guise of protecting Elspeth, even though he didn't know where she was and Henry was trying to appear suave as he scuttled under Cuthbert's kitchen table.

Ronald had entered tactical mode and every time this 'creature' lurched one way he prepared to dive the other, which resulted in several freeze-frame moments resembling the strobe-lighting at a disco.

Cuthbert simply stood his ground and watched the whole thing; he had been threatened by Percy's tractor in every way imaginable and somehow if he stood still, everything worked out for the best.

With a final clashing of gears and crunching of levers, the machine stopped just short of flattening him.

Cuthbert smiled at his own judgement, just as the massive head gave one last swing and knocked him flat on his back. Cuthbert glared up at the useless inanimate object and Percy glared back.

As the vibrating farm buildings settled down and the smoke cleared, everyone began to collect around the Valley's new occupant and listen to the adventures of Percy who was insisting upon being called Percy McTronic because there was no sign of Annie.

Henry was about to ask the question that no-one else wanted to be responsible for when blue flashing lights added to the surreal events and PC Beeching's patrol car screeched to a halt. Now all the attention switched to watching the overweight officer trying to squeeze out of his car to arrest the dinosaur.

"That's him," he gasped. "He escaped from the museum in the next valley breathing fire and smoke before crushing several police cars, why has he ended up here and why is Percy on its back?"

Percy pushed his goggles up onto the top of his head recreating the panda look he always achieved after tractor driving and said "This is part of a long tradition in my family officer, one of my ancestors, Terry Dactyl–Plumm was a dinosaur wrangler. That's why some of them had long necks, they wouldn't come quietly."

Beeching had been studying the creature and trying to figure out where to put his handcuffs when a breeze caused the huge head to swing and the teeth to clack. He gulped. "Go on," he said trying to figure out a way to take the credit for distracting the dinosaur by letting it eat Percy.

43

Percy continued, "That's why they built Stonehenge; it was a platform for presenting prizes after the dinosaur racing."

"You said it was a war memorial," pointed out the Captain.

Percy looked annoyed, "It's been around for ages; it was probably a bowling alley at some stage as well."

As the Captain tried to imagine bowling around in circles, Percy continued, "My family always had something special," he said ignoring the smirks from his audience "We were known as dinosaur whisperers."

"But they haven't got ears" pointed out Henry who had overheard Elspeth in the bar.

Percy raised himself in the saddle, or in this case his tractor seat to study the head in front of him. "Well, this one hasn't," he spluttered, "but a lot of the others had and they were the ones we whispered to."

"Which ones were they then?" asked a voice trying to not sound like Cuthbert.

Constable Beeching came to the rescue by insisting that "sore throats were common and even he had heard of hoarse whisperers but what he wanted to know was 'did Percy know anything about this dinosaur?"

Percy rummaged about in his welly and came out with a screwed up museum label which he studied, before announcing that it was a "Juvenile Triceratops whose horns hadn't fully formed and it was twenty feet long and weighed several tons."

Beeching had been licking his pencil and writing furiously, but he stopped to ask, "And he told you all that did he?" before closing his notebook and backing off as the dinosaur slowly nodded its head.

As the patrol car drove off, Jasper appeared from beneath the head and grinned at everyone.

Percy jumped down from his perch and asked "Any tea left?"

Chapter Fifteen

The women had convened a meeting in the Mandrake Arms and there was still plenty of enthusiasm for a tea-room and it was possible that things might even expand into a 'Jurassic Theme Park' under Geraldine's tutelage and enthusiasm, so there was plenty to talk about.

As everyone chatted animatedly, Elspeth noticed that Marjorie was strangely quiet. Leaning forward, she patted her friend's hand and asked what was wrong.

Marjory stirred from her reverie and replied "It's Percy, where does he keep appearing from when no-one in any of the shops ever sees him?"

The room went quiet until Arkle boomed "Why don't we ask him, he's just popped into that shop across the road."

Chairs scraped back as the ladies formed a posse and set out into the street to solve a mystery before dinner and ease Marjorie's curiosity.

Once again they had to split up and approach the shop from different directions, because no-one could quite pinpoint the right doorway.

Suddenly, Percy appeared amongst them and Arkle grabbed him from behind saying "Right you little twerp, what's going on?" and turned him to face everyone.

Percy stared at Arkle.

Arkle stared at Percy and backed off, the women gasped. Arkle had gone quite white and was stumbling her way back to the Mandrake Arms.

Percy gave a cheery "Good-day then ladies" and sauntered away, whilst the women looked from one to the other and back again in astonishment.

Marjorie watched him go and asked aloud, "What was that he was carrying?"

"A tomato plant, I think," replied Elspeth.

* * *

Back in the bar, the women clustered around their formerly invincible friend and the questions began.

45

"Are you alright Ar..?" asked Geraldine.

"Ar..?" snapped Arkle.

"Are we able to help?" interposed Marjorie wisely.

"Are you alright?" tried Elspeth.

Gradually Arkle calmed down until the twisted pewter tankard could be wriggled out from between her fingers and it sat on the table looking like a forlorn Barbara Hepworth sculpture.

Arkle sighed and looked around the concerned faces of her friends. She wasn't used to being on the receiving end of sympathy and this didn't come easily. "Did you see what he was carrying?" she asked.

"Tomatoes?" suggested Elspeth.

Arkle shuddered, causing her checked tweed to ripple like an earthquake on an ordnance survey map, "Yes, tomatoes, my Achilles heel."

"Allergic are we dear?" asked Marjorie with a puzzled look.

Arkle sighed and began to relate the tales of her mother drawing faces onto tomatoes when she was a child and surprising her at all times of day and night; sometimes it was a smiley face, sometimes a grumpy face and sometimes something that would only pass muster on Halloween. But it was the constant not knowing, what time, what face? That all combined to leave her a nervous wreck.

That was partly why she had become horse-mad, because she could be outside for hours and ride alone for miles and the bonus was that horses didn't eat tomatoes.

The ladies all made sympathetic noises and gradually wandered off; it wasn't nice to see an icon of non-femininity shrivel before your eyes.

* * *

Percy stood the tomato plant right in the centre of Cuthbert's kitchen table, so that he could walk around it and study it from all angles. He knew terror when he saw it, especially when terror had him in its vice-like grip and was shocked into letting go. He was sat at the table swinging his little legs when the men began to file in and everyone focused upon this unusual centrepiece.

"Hah," laughed Henry, "Don't let the daughter see that Percy, "your life won't be worth living."

Percy leaned forward eagerly, "Tell me more," he insisted.

Avril meanwhile had been accompanying Cuthbert on a tour of his graveyard; her editor had come up with the idea for a local interest story of interesting inscriptions on the headstones, so against her better judgement there she was halfway up a hill surrounded by a mish-mash of headstones all leaning in different directions and trying to get Cuthbert to remember why they were there. She had tried to get the local interest side from actual locals, but all they wanted to know was *where* any local might be buried.

Scraping the lichen from one of the stones, Avril reluctantly called Cuthbert over and pointed to an inscription stating "E Lord, she was thin"

"Why on earth would they mention whether she was fat or not?" asked the reporter.

Cuthbert remembered this one, the woman had been very religious and it should have said, "Lord she was thine" and when the family had pointed out that he had missed the 'e' off, he assumed that they were from Lancashire and put it on the front.

The rest of the family had simply refused to die whilst Cuthbert was still in charge and they were setting records for longevity.

Avril tried another tack, "When the old church was still in use did they have any relics of the Saints?"

"Oh yes," replied Cuthbert. "Ours were envied throughout the valleys and eventually they went to the main cathedral because ours were better than theirs." He said proudly.

"Such as?" as Avril thoroughly intrigued now.

Cuthbert looked around and whispered, "We had the skull of Saint Peter."

Avril paused before pointing out that the main cathedral already had that."

Cuthbert tapped the side of his nose and said, "Ahh, but ours was his skull as a young man."

Avril closed her Cuthbert-proof, non-spiral notebook and began to calculate the quickest way to civilisation before night fell, but Cuthbert was already weaving his way home instinctively.

Avril sighed and began to follow. As the shadows lengthened, Avril caught up with Cuthbert and attempted to make conversation because graveyards in the dark were simply imagination's way of allowing your childhood fears to resurface.

"Are you ever nervous out here in the dark Cuthbert?" she asked, resisting the temptation to link arms with him.

Cuthbert half turned and replied, "Only when prisoners escape and hide amongst the headstones."

Avril's eyes widened and her head swivelled like an owl. "Has that happened?" she asked with a gulp.

"Oh yes," smiled Cuthbert "the last one quickly changed his name and assumed a new identity; he was Miles O'Weigh when they caught him. The next one was caught at the orphanage trying to adopt de'se guys to help him escape."

Chapter Sixteen

Arkle leapt out of bed and swished the curtains open, ready to greet a new day and jump a few fences before breakfast.

Stretching her arms, she took in the view and froze. There, outside her window dangled a tomato with a big smiley face drawn on it. She swished the curtains closed again and trembled; somebody knew, her Achilles heel had been discovered. It seemed a long process getting dressed knowing that somewhere out there, someone knew.

Margery looked up in surprise as Arkle sneaked into the kitchen checking all the corners and lifting saucepan lids.

"I thought you were already out for a morning ride," tried Margery trying to ignore the odd behaviour.

Arkle didn't seem to hear her and instead asked a question of her own. "Have you seen anyone odd around here lately, Margery?" she asked.

It was Margery's turn to laugh, "Odd? In the valley, you'll have to narrow it down a bit dear."

Arkle was still on red alert when Margery added, "What the...?" just as Arkle turned and saw the top tomato in the vegetable basket grinning at her, she gave out a shriek and left.

* * *

Percy sat at Cuthbert's table trying to avoid washing the breakfast dishes, which wasn't difficult, because he was a past master at avoiding everything, but at least he seemed deep in thought.

When Henry, Ronald and the Captain entered, he didn't even look up and Cuthbert just shrugged at the unasked questions from everyone.

Eventually Henry asked, "Penny for your thoughts, Percy."

Percy looked up slowly and tapping his head replied, "Anything from up here would cost more than that matey."

Ronald snorted, "All I can see is a scruffy old cap sat on a prototype scarecrow; we would have to pay someone to take you away."

Percy glared, but stayed silent until the Captain asked "Come on Percy, what's taking all that concentration?"

Percy shuffled and replied, "Well if you must know, I'm thinking of taking a holiday."

"From what?" exploded from three different sources at once; "You don't *do* anything."

Percy waited for the incredulity to settle down, before he said, "It's just a matter of where to go; what luggage would I need for the last resort?"

* * *

Arkle was getting in quite a lather which was a reversal because that was usually the job of the horse. Diving into Avril's newspaper office, she took a chair opposite the reporter's desk where she could see the street and started to blather about writing an article showing all the horsey people where to ride in the Valley.

Even when Avril pointed out that there was only one horsey person in the Valley and she was sat opposite her right now, Arkle was still describing the children's route which was easy because she had already knocked most of the fences down.

Avril sighed and began to unwrap her lunch, there seemed to be a bigger variety than usual. "Well, would you look at that?" she said.

Arkle did indeed look at that tomato with a leering face drawn on it and she promptly fled.

Jasper was still recovering from almost being steamrollered by Arkle charging out of the newspaper office and he allowed himself a minute to remember what Margery's instructions had been.

It was basically, "Find out what that little twerp is up to and how does he disappear into a high street shop where I've spent all my life and never noticed it?"

Jasper continued his stroll. The shops looked slightly different walking one way down the street and again when you came back in the opposite direction and yet there was nothing you hadn't already seen. This called for an aerial view, thought Jasper and he gripped the nearest drainpipe to test it before starting to climb.

Chapter Seventeen

Percy, meanwhile had left Cuthbert's having successfully avoided hot water and all aspects of dishwashing and he was now tending to his tomato plants on top of the row of shops.

He hadn't planted them, but someone had and Percy was a great one for inheriting the produce of someone else's labours, so he snipped and he cut and he hummed away to himself. He frowned at the secateurs as if the power of his gaze would sharpen the blades for him and when this didn't work, he shook them vigorously.

Jasper had just released his grip on the drainpipe and gripped the edge of the roof to pull him over, when the secateurs slipped from Percy's hand and spiralled through the air, before rapping the mafia leader on the knuckles and sending him back to the street below.

* * *

The bar in the Mandrake arms was full when Percy took a rest from his labours and wandered in to join the throng.

The men were watching the pot-plant in the corner which seemed to have a bandage on one of its branches and it hissed dangerously when Percy entered.

The women meanwhile were watching Arkle as she checked behind curtains and under cushions as if something was lurking and only she knew what it was.

Percy sidled up to her and suddenly produced something from his welly with a conjuror's flourish.

Arkle shrieked and stepped back as Percy offered her…a plum.

The tension in the room was unbearable especially with half of the residents not knowing what was happening; a quarter of them having a good guess and the rest quite happy to misinterpret everything and just enjoy the show.

The Captain coughed and commented "Funny things crowds of people you know, ever heard of mass hysteria?" He only paused because he had no intention of stopping and then continued, "One person starting to panic can set everybody off. I remember when I was in a small village and the natives all began to yell and point and run

51

away, but of course we stood our ground and joked as if nothing was happening. Couldn't lose face in front of the Mem-sahibs you know."

"Well, was anything happening?" asked Henry.

The Captain paused before replying,

"Oh yes, old Carruthers was trampled by an elephant, a lion got Blenkinsop and a crocodile was dragging old Smithers away to make a handbag out of him."

The assembled men supped silently in an attempt to rationalise this tale of the Englishman abroad, when Percy contributed, "Fear takes on many guises my friends, but facing it alone is the real test. Did I tell you about my relation who hitch-hiked with the phantom motorist?"

Now, Percy's questions had the effect of causing everyone's pint to hesitate in mid-air, whilst they went through their mental filing systems looking for excuses, illnesses and excuses to not be there, but all that took time and meanwhile Percy had shuffled and signalled for lubrication in a glass.

"It was out in the country," Percy began, "Really rural and the car my relation had borrowed had skidded into a ditch, so he started to hitch-hike once he found the main road, but the rain was hammering down and the lightning caused the air to sizzle and the trees to close in eerily as the thunder rolled."

The bar had gone quiet and everyone began to close in around Percy and they were listening intently.

"Eventually," continued Percy, barely acknowledging another free pint, "A set of headlights appeared travelling in his direction, but due to the storm and the crashing confusion of the heavens, it seemed to take forever to reach him, but when it did, he snatched open the back door and dived in.

Shivering with cold, but ecstatic with relief, he looked up to thank the driver for the lift, but there was no-one there.

He was alone and the car continued to move forward silently as my relative tried to come to terms with it all.

"*Suddenly*," Percy banged his hand on the table making everyone jump. "The next flash of lightning showed a narrow bridge approaching and he was aiming straight at it. He tried to reach over the back of the seats, but it was too far and the bridge was getting closer and closer; he could see the brickwork and then suddenly he saw something else. A hand reached into the car and gripped the steering wheel; it didn't touch him or harm him, it simply gently steered the car away from danger and when the vehicle was back on a straight course, it disappeared.

Now my relative was glad to be saved, but he was terror-stricken and when he saw the lights of a hotel up ahead, he jumped out of the car and sprinted through the rain heading for safety.

Bursting into the bar, he blurted out his tale to the incredulous customers who took in his drenched clothing and sorry state and they began to cluster together for mutual support when the door opened and two more drenched customers entered and one of them pointed to my relative."

"What happened?" asked Avril "Had they seen the same ghost?"

"No," sighed Percy, "Apparently one of them said to the other, "There's that idiot who climbed into the car when we were pushing it."

The bar went quiet and Margery sighed at the sight of three empty glasses where Percy had been.

The silence didn't last long as Arkle screamed and crashed out taking tables and chairs with her and there, left behind in her haste was a cocktail glass with a cherry-tomato in it smiling at the world.

Chapter Eighteen

The men were convinced that the world was only put to rights around Cuthbert's kitchen table when they were in attendance, but the truth was that Elspeth's table was also the scene of the planning of great events like the creation of the new tea-room.

But sometimes, things became quite surreal, like the day when Elspeth regaled them with tales of magic she had witnessed in far off lands.

Avril had scoffed at the stories of transposition from men into animals and Elspeth had been stung, so she used her superior cleaning experience to announce in her best transcendental manner "Do you realise that when I clean the vacuum cleaner, I *become* the vacuum cleaner?"

Avril was unfazed, she sighed and replied, "Oh I sold mine, it was just gathering dust."

* * *

Jasper had succeeded in gaining the roof, where Percy tended to his tomato plants. He had climbed up right at the end of the row and edged along the ridge tiles, until he could drop onto a flat roof extension where Percy was lying in a deckchair with a huge newspaper opened out before him.

Percy flapped half of the broadsheet back and nodded to Jasper, before resuming his reading.

"You seem busy," said Jasper cautiously.

"Studying stocks," replied Percy absently.

This interested Jasper immensely as he handled the mafia's finances, "How are they doing?" he demanded excitedly.

Percy folded the newspaper carefully, before addressing his visitor, "Usual variations, I suppose Jasper. Aerospace is up, water is choppy, duck feathers are down and envelopes are stationary."

Jasper stared at his own feet and counted to ten to calm down, because he was much too pretty to go to prison. When he looked up, Percy was gone.

Constable Beeching meanwhile, was in the antique shop in the next valley where Martin Hepplewhite was trying to discreetly arrange some protection from the valley mafia.

"They're just kids," snorted the constable, "I've never locked one of them up."

Martin eyed the policeman's girth and muttered, "Only because you couldn't catch one."

Beeching was wandering around the shop, jeopardising every piece of stock. He came too close too, until Martin could stand it no more.

"Look officer, if I can be sure that you'll react instantly when I call, I'll make it worth your while."

Constable Beeching was appalled, his integrity had been challenged, "Don't you try those salesman tricks on me feller-me-lad, that Cuthbert once tried to sell me a coffin, but I didn't fall for it. It's the last thing I'll need," he snorted.

* * *

Margery had press-ganged Henry, Ronald and Percy into accompanying her to a supermarket in the next valley and they were merrily grumbling away as she passed them items to put into their various trolleys.

Passing some fruit and being deliberately irritating, she chirruped "An apple a day, keeps the doctor away."

Henry contributed, "An orange a day, keeps the taxman away."

"Does anything here, keep the nuts away?" asked Percy looking pointedly at Ronald who sneered, "So basically, throwing fruit at people gets you some peace eh?"

When the carts were full, Margery waited to pay and 'the boys' were allowed to wait for her outside.

Watching a council lorry go past with a huge hopper on the back, Percy shuddered.

"What's wrong?" asked Henry in a relaxed moment of weakness.

Percy looked distraught and replied, "My uncle was cycling to work and he skidded on the ice and fell off his bike as one of those things went past. He told us about it through gritted teeth."

Henry casually stepped in-between his brother and Percy before Margery spotted trouble brewing and refused to take them for ice cream.

Avril had taken herself up into the hills at the old end of the valley to get a sense of the atmosphere; it was probably the only sense she would ever get out of this valley.

It was a beautiful day and Avril sat on the hillside basking in the sun as she imagined the tramp of feet and the dragging of huge tails through the undergrowth.

The gentle wind rippled the leaves and made the grass sound like surf on a distant shore. The sounds were perfect and the atmosphere was sublime, Avril sighed, "All right Jasper, come on out, I know you're there."

Jasper appeared with a grin and sat beside her, "Have you seen the footprints yet?" he asked.

Margery watched as the taxi driver loaded the shopping into his boot and said brightly, "Just follow the main road and I will direct you as we go," she knew better than to give away her destination too early, until she had an escort provided by the valley mafia.

The men on the other hand had been left to enjoy some 'down-time' and finish their coffee, so as Henry paid, Percy strode up to the taxi rank, opened one of the doors and announced "To the next valley please my good man."

This resulted in a smell of burning rubber and Percy being left holding a car door handle in his hand.

"You berk," spluttered Ronald "how do we get home now?"

Once again, Henry stepped between them and asked, "Is that a bus over there?"

Avril had seen the footprints and explored the region with Jasper so that she could prepare a preliminary report on the attractions awaiting visitors to the Valley. They had found caves, artefacts and all sorts of primitive wall paintings; some of the paint was still wet.

As the tour came to an end, Jasper remembered Percy's animatronics dinosaur and off they went in search of it.

The bus driver was worried, this bus only ran once a year to keep the route through the Valley open and he usually put his foot down, closed his eyes and hurtled through as fast as he could.

It was up to the cleaners at the depot to peel all the sheepskin rugs off the front of the bus and this had long since become a topic no-one ever mentioned.

He chewed his fingernail and studied the three men before him, not only did they want to pay for tickets to the Valley; they wanted him to *stop* there.

The one doing all the talking seemed reasonable enough; he could almost have been a T.V. presenter.

The shorter one looked downright dangerous, he kept one hand in his pocket and was studying the driver as if he was reminding himself where all the major arteries were.

Behind them was a scruffy little twerp in turned down wellies who, on closer inspection had duct tape across his mouth. Perhaps it was a kidnapping, but if anyone would pay more than a turnip for the scruffy one, the bus driver would be very surprised.

He reluctantly opened the door with a hiss and they climbed gratefully aboard, sitting Percy right at the back out of earshot, so that he couldn't cause any more trouble, but once the engine roared into life, it obviously wouldn't be a problem.

Between the noise, the fumes and the destination, it was a wonder that the driver had survived this long.

Ronald reached over and took great delight in tearing the duct-tape from Percy's face; he could see Percy ranting, but it was all lost in the cacophony of the bus, pure heaven.

Avril stared, closed her eyes and then stared some more, there standing before her was a dinosaur on caterpillar tracks surrounded by the valley mafia all beaming as if they had just made it from cereal boxes. "Does it move?" breathed Avril.

She was rewarded with a collective, "Oh yes," from the mafia and Jasper was encouraged to climb up and demonstrate.

After the usual mind numbing ignition of the engine, the tracks began to clatter as Jasper eased left and right causing the head to sway from side to side.

With yelps of delight, everyone including Avril climbed aboard and the adventure began.

Now, with caterpillar tracks, the wrong type of mud on the wrong type of slope can cause some spectacular complications so although the adventure had begun, there was no way of telling where it would end.

Percy was still rubbing his face where the duct tape had been. Unfortunately, just as Ronald had applied it, Percy had stuck his tongue out at him, so now his tongue was sticking to the roof of his mouth with the glue residue and Henry was trying to decipher the words he thought Percy was using over the engine noise.

Chapter Nineteen

Outside The Mandrake Arms, a terrified taxi driver was trying to look in all directions at once as he unloaded Margery's shopping, he almost dropped one of the bags when a distant horn sounded and a black and white sheepdog started to go berserk rounding up some sheep and herding them into the road.

The sound of the horn was joined by a squeal of brakes as the driver belatedly remembered that he was supposed to stop this time causing his passengers to slide down the bus ending up with their faces pressed against the windscreen just in time to see a dinosaur crash through the undergrowth and attack the bus head-on, trapping a mysterious delivery of sheepskin rugs in between them.

The bus gave a final sigh and its door sagged open allowing he passengers to stagger onto the road.

The mafia had disappeared leaving Avril perched high in the driving seat of a dinosaur which seemed to be trying to catch a bus.

Watching Percy waving his arms about without making a sound, Avril assumed that she had gone deaf and allowed herself to be led away into the bar.

The bus driver was put into the taxi whose driver waived his fee and set a new land-speed record for leaving the valley.

Percy jumped up and down on his hat in an attempt to free his tongue from the roof of his mouth because nothing happened in the Valley without his version of events.

The mafia had already laid the sheepskins out to dry and begun dismantling the bus and Blind Pugh had returned to his kennel. The wind sighed as the Valley returned to an approximation of normal.

* * *

Margery had assembled her council of war. Around the table sat Arkle, Avril, Geraldine and Elspeth. The tea was poured, the biscuits were allocated and the meeting could begin.

"Ladies, Percy has managed to find an unoccupied property on the main street. This would be perfect for our tea-room and allow us to run The Mandrake Arms as well. We need to watch him ladies and then squash him."

Arkle was appalled, she had been on the alert for rampant tomatoes and only half heard, "I'm not washing the scruffy little Herbert."

Margery sighed, "Squash him dear; not wash him."

A tremor went around the table as Arkle murmured "You can count me in then."

* * *

Percy paused and watched the reflections in the shop windows to see if anyone was watching and then he sidled sideways into a doorway set at an angle to the others. He had found it by accident some time ago when he had to quickly hug the shadows when Arkle was looking for him.

Slipping inside the shop, he paused again and breathed in deeply; the aromas gathered together into one olfactory stream of consciousness. Mahogany counters, brass screws, beeswax, iron fittings and sawdust all contained enticingly in little drawers with labels on them, for Percy this was paradise, a man was only as good as his parts he thought and there were enough parts here to build an Ark.

* * *

Cuthbert still hadn't solved the riddle of Percy's whereabouts and by the looks on the faces of the ladies around his kitchen table, neither had anyone else.

He looked from one scowl to the other and thought happy thoughts hoping that someone, somewhere needed some darning done and they would all dash away to the emergency.

The scowls deepened and the shadows lengthened, just knowing Percy was enough to bring biblical retribution to your door and eventually after keeping his head down for ages, Cuthbert sighed and announced "Oh all right, what do you want to know ladies?"

After being met by silence, he looked up and found himself quite alone with the revelation that 'Huh, happy thoughts really do work,' and he went to put the kettle on.

Chapter Twenty

The ladies were muttering and murmuring their way home in the dusk and Margery was trying to be logical. "Where did we last see turnip head?" she asked.

"Beside the bus after he had glued his mouth shut and just before Blind Pugh attacked him for treading on his tail" replied Elspeth.

"Did he cry for help?" asked a concerned Avril.

"Mouth-glued-shut," prompted Arkle.

"Oh," said Avril.

* * *

Cuthbert looked up in surprise as Percy entered the kitchen. "Where have you been?" he asked only mildly curious.

Percy tipped his hat back and placed his hands flat on the table as he stared at Cuthbert. "Don't try clever interrogation techniques on me mate, I know the women have been here and they will have told you what questions to ask. It won't work you know, because I'm not gullible."

Cuthbert laughed, "Of course you're not gullible, he was the chap who went on his travels and got himself tied up by all those little people."

Percy stared then gave up and went to bed.

* * *

Arkle was beginning to twitch; it was murder not knowing where she would see the next smiley-faced tomato and even her horse had taken to looking around corners and under jumps before committing itself.

Being on horseback gave her the advantage of being able to see over garden walls and look for secret crops and illicit greenhouses.

It was obviously Percy who was responsible, but where was his source? What was his distribution network? Were foreign strains being smuggled into the valley from tomato cartels across the world?

Arkle was suddenly very aware that she was the mounted warrior at the forefront of the tomato wars and she eased back on the reins blocking the main road into the Valley. "None shall pass." She intoned.

The valley mafia were getting confused, was Percy trying for a monopoly on vegetables and Arkle was a rival, or was there something hidden in the tomatoes?

They had already noticed a variety of faces on the ones they had retrieved, but there was nothing in the smiley faced one to make you happy and nothing in the sad face to have the relevant effect.

It seemed that Arkle was waiting for a fresh shipment on the main road, but Percy was propagating a small amount.

Perhaps he was controlling the market thought Jasper, and just releasing a small amount to control demand. Either way, these two needed to be watched. Secretly, Jasper was slightly embarrassed because the mafia had never seen a source of profit in vegetables.

Ronald had relaxed quite a bit lately and he was starting to see all the activity around Percy as a challenge; perhaps, it was time to settle scores? With all these people looking for him, how would Beeching know who had bumped him off; perhaps, it was time to do some of his own investigating?

Percy had a birds-eye view from his roof and he could see the mafia checking doors and windows; he could also see Arkle mounting guard on her horse further up the road like some bronze monument.

The worrying bit was when Ronald joined in though, some of his detection equipment was really sophisticated, or it had been before Percy slipped it into Margery's washing machine amongst some towels and then switched the machine on.

He watched Ronald kicking a really complicated piece of technology to get it to work before skimming it dangerously close to Blind Pugh.

* * *

Margery concluded the briefing around a table in the Mandrake Arms, stood up, and began to lead her troops across the road.

She was flanked by Elspeth on one side and Geraldine on the other, Avril brought up the rear with her notebook open. She was there purely as an observer, because she didn't actually have anything against Percy. Now, if it had been Cuthbert, she would have gone home for her steel toe-capped boots.

The women split up into pairs and walked towards each other studying the shop fronts.

As they came near to each other, they met in the middle none the wiser, there simply wasn't another doorway. They even tried it again counting door-knobs with the same result.

Margery didn't like mysteries, especially on her own doorstep and especially when it thwarted her own plans and most of all, when it involved *Percy*.

Chapter Twenty-One

The Captain and Henry were heading towards Cuthbert's and comparing notes about the way things had slowed down in the Valley. They found that their observations were remarkably similar, but of course they would be because they did the same things at the same time with the same people.

At least Cuthbert's kitchen was a constant and safe as long as you didn't sit too close to the cooking range or on the flight path of knives thrown by Ronald at Percy.

Cuthbert looked pathetically pleased to see them, but Henry and the Captain were having trouble seeing *him*.

"What the devil," spluttered the Captain, "This brings back my jungle training; quick, pass me a machete and check your boots for tarantulas."

Henry placed a hand on his friends elbow to calm him down as he tried to spot Cuthbert amongst the dozens of tomato plants.

"I take it Percy has hidden his crop where no ladies have ever ventured to dust?" he said.

A plant moved and Cuthbert was suddenly closer to the kitchen range and the kettle gave a hiss.

Another plant on the other side of the room moved to announce the secret presence of the mafia in listening mode.

"Oh come on out Jasper and have a cup of tea with us," sighed Henry.

Jasper stepped into view and replied, "Not a chance mate, I've seen him cleaning his tractor with it and it sparkled like new afterwards."

Henry and the Captain subtly pushed their cups away.

The Captain broke the silence with, "What's happening Cuthbert, where's Percy these days?"

Cuthbert took a sip of his tea and ignored the looks of horror as he swallowed it. Nodding towards Henry, he said, "It's all his fault, he gave Arkle some sort of tomato complex as a child and Percy is getting his revenge for all the time she has either trampled him or used him as a dishcloth."

Henry was appalled, "Nothing to do with me," he insisted. I was abroad at the time."

"At the time of what?" asked Cuthbert.

Henry looked around wildly, "Everything, I made sure of that," he blustered.

Cuthbert sighed, "Well as usual, I'm stuck with all of this lot. If Arkle finds it, I'm in trouble and then there's Percy's sulking, so at the moment I'm holding my breath."

How can she possibly find out?" asked Henry hopefully glancing around at all the tomato plants.

Jasper giggled and looking around him said, "She'll hear it on the grapevine."

* * *

The women were still walking up and down the High Street in different directions and suddenly turning in the hope of catching a shop-front jumping back into line, but no-one was having any luck, so with a concerted sigh, they gathered around Margery who held a handful of high denomination notes in the air and announced "Right, this is the reward, the first one to spot the little twerp gets it.

"Thank you," said Jasper snatching the money and starting to count the notes.

"A reward doesn't work like that Jasper," snapped Margery trying to grab the money back, "You have to know where he is."

"Oh, Ok" replied Jasper still counting, "He's over there" and he nodded towards the Mandrake Arms where Percy was just disappearing inside.

The women gave a communal snarl and crossed the street like a coven of witches finding a new cauldron store.

Chapter Twenty-Two

Belinda had been tending the bar all morning before the men started to appear. She wasn't happy at being disturbed, because looking after a bar where Margery kept everything spotless was just about the limit of her skills.

If Margery found a way to polish glass any harder, they would need a new shade of transparent.

Henry and Ronald had been served and sat down and then the Captain joined them, closely followed by Cuthbert who joined the others at a table. He had no sooner sat down than Percy appeared and everyone had to move sideways to make room for him.

Now, everyone else was wise to this strategy, except Cuthbert who moved his chair and sat looking at a space where his drink had been and then he looked at Percy who was licking his lips and putting an empty glass down.

Everyone sniggered quietly as Cuthbert fetched another drink and sat with both hands wrapped around the glass.

While this was going on, only Belinda noticed the women begin to file in silently, surrounding the table and covering the exits.

Percy was just holding forth upon the subject of evolution, "And I'll tell you another creation myth," he said, "It's not true that when God made the flamingo he was making storks, but he left a red sock in the machine."

He sat back waiting for a free pint to appear from somewhere and noticed that his audience was strangely quiet and then he noticed that he couldn't see through the door onto the street. Then he smelled horse.

Margery slowly circled the table like a stoat fixing them all with her stare, it was never good to dive straight in and quiz the twerp you needed the answers from.

First, you had to unsettle the followers and isolate the leader. "So, Cuthbert," she began, "I thought we could practice for when this place becomes a restaurant and tea-room." She paused for effect before adding "Unless of course we find somewhere else to lay our gingham table-cloths."

Cuthbert looked around wildly, why had she picked on him? The nearest he had been to a restaurant had been on a trip to another valley when he stopped at a burger van and accidentally kicked the wedge out from under the wheel and was forced to watch his hot-dog, the caravan and its owner hurtling downhill away from him. Arguably, he could claim to have invented fast food.

Margery had enrolled Avril as the pretend waitress and she hovered at Cuthbert's shoulder with her notebook open and Cuthbert was instantly distracted by imagining himself running along the shiny spiral at the top of it. This always produced a dreamy look as if Cuthbert wasn't quite at home when they needed him to be.

"Well Cuthbert," asked Margery sweetly "What will it be?"

A distracted Cuthbert held up his empty glass.

Margery sighed patiently, "The pub has gone Cuthbert, you are ordering in a restaurant now, how may we help you?"

Cuthbert replied dreamily, "a table for two please."

Margery was delighted, "There you go Avril, a table for two people please dear."

Cuthbert became alert, "No, not two people."

"You said table for two," growled Margery in a dangerously low voice.

"Yes, two O'clock" said Cuthbert nodding.

"Well, how many for?" hissed Avril joining in.

"Yes" confirmed Cuthbert.

"Yes what?" screamed Avril.

"Four," whispered Cuthbert, hesitantly feeling the mood change.

"For what?" yelled Avril and Margery in unison.

"For dinner?" tried Cuthbert meekly.

The women stared at each other; the whole idea had been to soften up the men and then grind Percy down into revealing where his mysterious shop was, but when they came out of the Cuthbert induced reverie, the table was empty and the men were gone.

Percy had slipped into his shop, whilst no-one was looking and he was humming cheerfully as he opened one little mahogany drawer after another. They were all labelled on the fronts with the names of all the necessities such as tacks, nails, screws, rivets and hinges. For Percy, this was indeed heaven.

Cuthbert's barns held all manner of heavy equipment and big hammers, but this was where the finishing touches were found. Still humming, he remembered that some foreigner had once said, "Give me a lever long enough and I can move the Earth."

Percy snorted and muttered, "Give me a big enough battery and I'll make it spin on it own."

Margery was struggling to calm down, but even she knew that the pub glasses wouldn't take another rigorous polishing, so she took all the logs out of the fireplace and dusted them instead. Elspeth was right, she thought dusting was therapeutic, it gave you time to think up some really nasty tortures.

Chapter Twenty-Three

Meanwhile, the men were back at Cuthbert's farm and there was only one topic of conversation; where was Percy and what was he up to?

Actually, that was two topics and when the plant in the corner asked, "Is there a reward?" and Ronald threw a chair at it, only to discover that Jasper was standing behind him, the whole thing descended into chaos with Cuthbert opening the cooking range door to let a jet of flame out to separate the warring parties.

Margery eyed Jasper warily as he sat at the bar nursing an orange juice like a melancholic old man with his life behind him. "I can't get used to seeing you sat there Jasper" she said, "It doesn't seem two days since you were too young to come in for a drink and yet now, here you are sitting there."

The sarcasm was equally mixed with affection as he was the king-pin of her valley mafia and it was obvious that something was troubling him.

Jasper made eye contact at last and asked, "You know that nut-job who runs the museum?"

Margery was taken aback, "Now then Jasper, have some respect, she's the most educated person in the Valley, I think she has three degrees."

Jasper snorted, "The only way she could end up with three degrees was if she found a thermometer." He paused, "We've been watching her and Percy has been watching her and Ronald has been watching her...."

Margery held up a hand and asked "What's your point Jasper, the valley is boring and we're all watching each other?"

Jasper took a delicate sip of his orange juice and eyed Margery carefully, before replying, "Not *all* of us Margery, you seem more interested in Percy and the mafia have been fully tasked following *him* around." He paused again before adding, "You know exactly where that shop is, don't you Margery? Geraldine has been loose and unsupervised for all this time. I hope there's nothing going on, which could affect the future mafia profit margins."

Margery bristled, her emotions followed the route of all adults caught out trying to trick the up and coming, she blushed, she blustered, she almost threatened, but the slurping sound as Jasper finished his drink

acted like a punctuation mark and her shoulders slumped.

"You're right" she acceded, "It's the old ironmonger's shop, due to the angle of the windows and a trick of the reflection in the glass, you can walk past it in both directions without seeing it.

Percy must have stumbled against the door, or something." "Having purchased intoxicating liquor from an unknown source, no doubt," said Jasper sarcastically, before realising that this was a step too far and asking, "Why didn't he use the tunnel?"

Margery had been about to blast Jasper with a verbal broadside, but she deflated again, "What tunnel?" she asked.

They both knew that the Valley was undermined by various tunnel systems, some of which began as water supplies and drainage, but all of them had become a highway system for the mafia and even the locals when it was raining heavily.

Jasper accepted a top-up of his drink, the way he'd seen Percy do it when there was an advantage to be played, before stating "The one leading across here and coming out behind the fireplace."

* * *

Percy had scuttled back to Cuthbert's farm with his pockets full of nuts and bolts and he was swarming all over his new toy which he still insisted upon calling Annie.

The animatronics dinosaur had responded well to its controls and Percy was working on a sound system. There was no electricity in the Valley, so rechargeable batteries were not an option and the mafia's monopoly on the supply of batteries made that difficult too.

He had brought up the situation at the last meeting at Cuthbert's house where he had demanded action and thumped the table shouting, "Are we men or mice?"

He was answered by the way everyone scuttled off, because Percy had forgotten that Jasper was hidden behind the plant in the corner.

Still, to Percy a problem was simply an opportunity to pass it on to someone else and he had abandoned all thoughts of batteries when he found a wind-up gramophone in Cuthbert's attic.

He was now sat on top of Annie the dinosaur, furiously winding the handle before placing a record on the turntable.

Ronald, the Captain and Henry were approaching steadily and they veered towards the dinosaur to see what he was up to just as Percy dropped the needle on the record and let out the clutch.

The strains of "Nellie the Elephant" blasted out from the newly installed speakers and the monstrosity began to move forward picking up speed as it went.

The cacophony was awesome; it drove out all thoughts of the now and encouraged fresh thoughts of the then.

Ronald reached for the gun he hadn't got; Henry reached for his reporter's notebook and came up blank as well, whilst the Captain adopted the pose he had used to stop stampeding elephants.

* * *

Sat around Cuthbert's table, the three of them were trying to stop the ringing in their ears and the shaking in their legs, which wasn't necessarily just vibration.

Ronald was convinced that he could have "Put one straight between its eyes."

Henry would have been happy with a Pulitzer Prize for reporting it and the Captain was convinced that his technique still worked.

Cuthbert was pouring the tea and Percy was sat on the rocky three-legged stool which was the equivalent of the naughty step. "Nobody ever notices the advances in technology" he muttered. "Oh no, all they see is that they were standing in the wrong place at the wrong time and it was someone else's fault. He couldn't hold it in any longer, so he addressed everyone, "When one of my ancestors' lands on Mars, there'll be one of you clots in the way, that's why there were footprints on the moon."

Henry blinked, before he replied, "There were footprints on the moon because the astronauts had already had a walk around."

Percy glared, "That's what they tell you, but my family has ancient moon maps proving that we got there first."

The room was quiet, they were used to Percy claiming historical achievements, but this seemed different somehow.

"Have you still got them?" asked Henry cautiously.

71

"Of course I have" snapped Percy "I can be trusted with my families heritage; it even shows the area we explored."

"Well," said Ronald in a mock whisper "If Percy's lot were there, it wouldn't be in the sea of tranquillity."

Everyone sniggered and Percy stomped away. He could be heard banging and thumping in the far reaches of the house before returning exultantly with a cardboard tube under his arm. "There," he said triumphantly sliding out a rolled up map and weighting the corners down with various cups. "What do you say to that?"

Henry answered slowly, "I'd say that it's the same map that all schoolchildren were given to commemorate the event."

Percy gasped, "How dare you, how do you explain the territory marked out and shaded in brown?"

"Coffee stain?" suggested the Captain.

Chapter Twenty-Four

Margery was not her usual self; she had gathered the other women in the bar of The Mandrake Arms to announce that things weren't quite going to plan.

"There's a plan?" asked Arkle who missed a lot of meetings due to jumping over fences, especially when she was looking for her horse.

Margery gritted her teeth; she didn't like to admit defeat or even being suspected of near defeat. "The mafia know about the old hardware shop where the tea-room is going to be and they are suspicious of Geraldine and her activities. We won't have the free rein on this project that we had hoped for ladies, because the mafia will demand a cut and the men-folk will somehow convince themselves that it was all their idea."

Arkle scoffed "The men are no problem Margery, do you know how many horses disappear every year?"

Margery tried to keep up, "What do horses have to do with men dear?"

Arkle sat back and waved a hand dismissively "Same thing, just twice as many legs."

* * *

Jasper had called an emergency meeting which resulted in most of his 'men' sitting there looking like chipmunks, because he had interrupted their tea and they were still chewing. "Everybody in this Valley is up to something" announced Jasper causing his men to swallow hard and look at each other suspiciously. "Not you lot," said Jasper in exasperation, "All the others."

That didn't clear the air at all; it just made everybody move away from everybody else, in case they were the 'other lot.'

Jasper sighed, sometimes he couldn't see the benefits of high command, but in a last attempt, he stated "The grown-ups, the grown-ups are up to something."

After various questions, the puzzled looks continued until one brave soul timidly ventured, "But we know all that Jasper, there's going to be a tea-room and a dinosaur themed amusement park where we dress as those brown furry things and get stuff for people."

"Brown furry things?" stammered Jasper, "What are you talking about?"

Someone else spoke up and said "He's right boss, we were listening in as you said and the women are going to dress us as gophers and make us fetch things."

Jasper gasped, he had left a team behind the fireplace listening to the women's meeting. "So," he spat "They think they can use the mafia as go-fors and servants, do they? We run this valley and its time to remind everyone of that."

Chapter Twenty-Five

In the bar later, Percy was still smarting over his moon-map. He couldn't understand it, because he distinctly remembered his mother saying that she'd given his father a rocket after he came up with some hair-brained scheme.

He watched the others around the table for a while and then asked "Did I tell you about..?"

Everyone looked around in panic, but at that moment Arkle entered, smelling of wet horse, so it was obviously raining outside and everyone slumped in their seats, waiting for the inevitable.

The inevitable was actually delayed until someone put a drink in front of Percy and he had shuffled sufficiently to get comfortable. "Have any of you heard the story of King Arthur and his sword?" he asked.

"Ahh," A voice was heard from the next table where the women had gathered, "The Morte de Arthur" said Geraldine.

Percy scoffed, "Mortars hadn't been invented yet; it was a sword."

Geraldine snorted, "It was a reworking of the round table tales by Sir Thomas Mallory."

"Who's telling this story?" snapped Percy causing Geraldine to roll her eyes up in their sockets and take a drink.

Percy watched her suspiciously for a while until Henry prompted "Excalibur?"

Percy grumbled "I know what I'd *like* to do to her."

Henry tried again, "no Percy, the sword Excalibur."

Percy roused himself, "Have I ever mentioned that my family made some of the finest swords in the world?"

"Cutlass?" suggested Ronald.

Percy looked at him in astonishment, "Of course they would cut a lass, they were razor sharp, that's why it was a man's trade."

Geraldine made an attempt to comment, but Margery and Elspeth laid a gentle hand over hers and she took the hint.

Percy continued. My family's tradition of sword making went back much further than that and we made Excalibur before setting it into the stone ready for Mordred to pull it free and become the King of England."

Both Henry and Geraldine interrupted at this point "Mordred? But it was Arthur who pulled the sword free and became King."

Percy shuffled and forced himself to admit that "I said we were great sword-smiths, I never said we were good with cement.

Mordred had put down a deposit on the sword with the intention of paying the rest when he was King, but this twerp Arthur needed a sword for a tournament and when he leant against it, the sword fell over, so he picked it up."

"But Mordred had paid for it?" clarified Henry.

Percy sagged a little, "Partly, that's why they were always fighting back then; he was trying to get it back because it was part of the plan to get him on the throne."

Cuthbert had been listening in fascinated silence, which was always a bad sign and he joined in now. "Is this the one where Arthur was dying and someone threw Excalibur into a lake?"

Percy nodded sadly as he accepted another pint. "In the final battle, Arthur was wounded and Mordred saw the sword and shouted 'Give it back,' so Arthur gave it back...point first.

With Mordred dead and himself mortally wounded, Arthur's last wish was for one of his Knights, Sir Bedevere to take Excalibur and throw it into the lake. The first time he only pretended because he knew a good sword when he saw one, but the second time a hand appeared, caught the sword and disappeared beneath the surface."

Percy waited dramatically for the applause, but Cuthbert wasn't finished "Who was it?" he asked excitedly, "Who was the lady in the lake?"

Percy frowned at the interruption and waved a hand dismissively "Oh, that was the sword-smiths mum; Arthur hadn't kept up the repayments."

The men sat contentedly at their table and Henry began to shuffle a set of dominoes, but Percy couldn't concentrate, he was struggling to see the table. It seemed darker at his end and that smell of wet horse hadn't gone away at all.

He suddenly jumped as Arkle boomed out from behind him, "Didn't we want to talk to this little twerp, Margery?"

Percy felt a hand on his shoulder and felt his spine compress.

76

Margery let him stew for a while before saying "It's alright dear, we have an arrangement now. Percy is giving up the old ironmonger's shop so that we can have a tea-room there and that will leave this bar as somewhere for the reprobates to gather."

Percy tried to stand up and protest, but between pressure from Arkle and glares from the men, he relaxed, after all he had never been promoted to reprobate before.

Chapter Twenty-Six

The women wandered into the lounge and Margery tried to check the fireplace for a secret tunnel. It was embarrassing because she had lived in the Valley all her life and this must be the only tunnel left. She was an expert on tunnels, priest holes and mouse holes, so she began rapping and tapping on the ancient wood panelling around it until something rapped back. "That's enough Jasper," she snarled and the rapping stopped but Margery was convinced that she had heard a muffled chuckle.

Returning her attention to the women, Margery came straight to the point, "We can't exclude either the men or the mafia, the Valley has always been a team effort and it will have to be now. If we can only trust Cuthbert to sell tickets, at least he's doing something."

Geraldine stretched and yawned "Well, he is the local undertaker, perhaps he can take care of people dying to get in?" she suggested.

Black humour, it was just what the women needed, thought Margery, the men in line, the mafia on board and the women on top. That was the natural order in the Valley.

There was no real need to discuss separate roles for the women, Margery oversaw operations and channelled the profits, Avril the local reporter would handle the publicity using information gleaned from Geraldine the archaeologist. Elspeth was more than happy to provide refreshments and dust the dinosaurs and Belinda the barmaid suffered from a nose-bleed if she came out from behind the bar and it went without saying that Arkle would be the muscle, so that left the men selling tickets.

The men however were seeing things rather differently, Henry with his television announcers voice would handle the tours and voice-overs using data stolen from the museum by Jasper.

The Captain would use his military experience to regiment the queues and keep them moving forward, especially if a dinosaur escaped and they needed a distraction.

Rodney would be in charge of security; his experiences as a mercenary would come in really handy because he was a great judge of people; basically, he would have a large mirror at the entrance and anyone who didn't look like *him* would be highly suspect.

Percy would be kept out of sight and supplied with oily cloths in case anything broke down and Cuthbert? Well, someone had to sell tickets didn't they?

The biggest problem was going to be planning something like this on a large scale. The days of just providing a walk-through exhibition with information signs were long gone. Should they base it on a ghost train where the public sat in carriages and the dinosaurs appeared between the trees?

Percy had assured everyone that he could lay miles of track through the Valley, taking it into caves and then looping the loop on the way back. It was at just about that point that his co-planners began to wander off.

Geraldine actually faced the same problem, because originally she had fallen into a hole and found the footprints in a tunnel or old river bed. Do you send people down to see them, or do you raise that part of the tunnel for easy access?

Either way, using Percy and his tractor was hardly straight out of the archaeological handbook was it?

This thing was also giving Jasper headaches; he'd had so many lately that he had begun to suspect that they were age related.

"Ok," He said, addressing his 'men' "It's obvious that the women generally know what they're doing because we've been through all this stuff before. Anyway, how hard can it be serving cream buns and cups of tea?"

He watched his lower ranking mafia nodding obediently and then added, "It's the men we've got to watch, they all have delusions of grandeur.

We've got a washed up T.V. announcer still living in his past, there's a Captain of lord-only-knows what living even further in *his* past.

As for that lean, mean fighting machine dopey Ronald, whoever's been paying him to be a mercenary needs a refund.

I suppose Percy does at least keep the greased wheels turning," he admitted, begrudgingly.

"What about Cuthbert?" asked a voice from the back, Jasper thought for a second before shrugging and replying "somebody has to sell tickets I suppose?"

The men were still in the bar of The Mandrake Arms because that's where men went to avoid women and their unholy knack for finding unnecessary work.

Henry couldn't help himself, he was still sniggering at Percy's tale of the Knights of the Round Table, but Cuthbert wasn't amused. "Huh" he snorted, "I sometimes think I'm related to Merlin the Magician"

"Why?" Asked Henry, bemused.

"Because every time I need help with something, people disappear," replied Cuthbert glaring at Percy.

In the next room, the ladies were ticking off items needed for the tea-rooms and Avril suggested having a flag above it.

"Where would we find a flag dear?" asked Margery curiously.

Arkle chimed in with "Didn't Hapless and Hopeless bring one back from the crematorium that day?"

Elspeth shivered at the memory, "Oh don't mention crematoriums, it means you won't have a body in the after-life and you will have to roam forever."

"Is that where ghosts come from?" asked Avril wide eyed.

Margery smiled, "Ronald says that it's to do with Cuthbert's filing system, nobody knows where they have been buried."

Henry had just announced that they would have to pay a visit to Marvin Middlewick at the Local Authority to check on planning permissions and things.

Percy was quite pleased, he rather liked the road gang, they were like him, and they thought that "Hi Jean" was a greeting and not a bar of soap.

Henry leaned forward conspiratorially and confided that one of the road gang had been sacked.

"Which one?" asked everyone at once, Henry waved a hand and said "none of the ones we knew, it was a new chap and he had been stealing.

"How did they find out?" asked Ronald, knowing full well it was usually the mafia at fault.

Henry sat back and said with a shrug "stuff had been going missing for a while and when they visited his house, all the signs were there."

It wasn't often Henry got the better of them and he thoroughly enjoyed the moment, especially when Percy was forced to respond with "Well, I was sacked from an orange juice factory because I couldn't concentrate."

Chapter Twenty-Seven

Marvin Middlewick sat contentedly behind his desk and surveyed his domain.

He had a hat stand in the corner, a large blotting pad on his desk and a sign which read C.L.O.S.E.D. The gilt letters actually stood for Council Liaison Office Supervising Excavations & Digging, but when anyone entered carrying armfuls of paperwork, they saw the sign, gasped, "Oh, sorry" and left.

There was no chair, because Marvin found that visitors spent so long looking around for it they forgot why they had come in and once again left.

After a timid knocking, a new office junior stuck her head inside his door making sure that her feet didn't cross the threshold and stuttered, "Are you expecting to give a television interview today Sir?"

Marvin tried to hide his surprise behind a coughing fit and then asked why she had brought it up.

The girl hesitated before blurting out, "Well Sir, we've just seen that news reporter crossing the yard; we used to see him on the T.V. all the time.

Marvin relaxed, he liked Henry, he was the only person he could relax with, and he might even kidnap the office junior's chair for the occasion.

Marvin smiled "So, did he have his crew with him?"

The girl hesitated, "Most of us thought it was a scarecrow Sir."

Marvin slumped down in his chair and asked "Where are they now?"

"Heading for the Drains Inspector's office, Sir," and almost with a curtsey she left.

"Watcher gang!" shouted Percy as he kicked the door open and charged into the office block set aside for the road gang.

They had been re-housed in this block, but their filthy profession which involved holes, mud, tunnels and drains meant that everything they touched showed handprints or footprints, so the floor was covered in newspapers and the walls were covered in safety posters.

It had started out just the odd poster here and there where someone had stumbled, but by now every inch was covered. It was like those hoardings where the poster for the new show covers the poster for the last one and over the years, the end result is an insane collage.

The road gang had jumped a foot at the shock of Percy's entrance, the fake radioactive sign on the door usually kept everyone away.

The gang were sitting at a table, playing cards. One lung Louie was gasping in shock, swivelling Simon was having trouble stopping his good eye rolling and getting it to line up with his glass one and Buster hadn't reacted at all.

When it came to panicking, Cuthbert and Buster could represent their country in showing absolutely no reaction at all, until it simply didn't matter anymore.

The Drains Inspector straightened up the cards and ignoring Percy, greeted Henry who had entered behind him. "Long time, no see Henry, care for a game of bridge?"

Henry was delighted; he hadn't played a civilised card game since he came to the Valley, so he gratefully took the seat vacated for him by Swivelling Simon.

Henry rubbed his hands together as if it would revitalise some kind of muscle memory and get him back to championship form. He waited for the cards to be dealt and then checked his hand, he gasped, it was the finest hand he had ever been dealt, the others began to lay their cards down and Henry was slightly puzzled at the way the cards were lining up towards each other but surely nothing could beat *his* hand?

After mentally reviewing his strategy, Henry made to lay down a card, but the Drains Inspector gave a sharp intake of breath and gently shook his head.

Henry was shocked, every time he tried to play a card the Inspector shook his head so Henry meekly said "Pass" and waited for the next turn. The two lines of cards were advancing towards each other and were very close now and as soon as there was a one card gap, Buster suddenly slammed a card down and shouted "Bridge."

Henry couldn't hold himself back any longer, "That's ridiculous; that's not how you play the game."

The Drains Inspector gave Henry a pitying look as he collected the cards up, "Never had you pegged for a sore loser" he said.

"I'm not," protested Henry, "But that's not how you play bridge."

Everyone stared at Henry as the Drains Inspector wearily explained "We're a road gang Henry, which makes us Civil Engineers, we lay the cards down in succession and the last card joins them together like a bridge…that's why it's called Bridge. Why else would anyone call a game *Bridge*?"

Henry gasped and noticed that the Inspector was using the same expression that Percy used when rhyme and reason left the room and someone had to take charge.

Henry stood up in a daze and headed for Marvin's office leaving the road gang shuffling the cards and Percy standing too close to the water cooler and wondering why his wellies were over -flowing.

* * *

Cuthbert didn't have many flights of fancy, that airport had closed long ago but as he sat alone in his kitchen, he began to realise how uniquely qualified he was for this new enterprise, after all, he multi-tasked as an undertaker and successful farmer without much trouble.

He could handle staff management, financial takings and accounting and have Blind Pugh on security detail.

He could even plan the tour routes; wait until he told everybody about the huge cave full of wall paintings.

At that moment, Percy kicked the door open and it kicked him back because it wasn't a soft touch like the one on the Drains Inspector's Office.

Percy stumbled in with water sloshing over the tops of his wellies and glared at the door as it closed behind him with an insolent creak.

Cuthbert was jumping up and down in excitement at the prospect of his new career and he revealed his plans to Percy.

Percy studied his friend for a moment before asking "Staff Management skills eh?"

Cuthbert nodded enthusiastically.

"Where are your chickens?" asked Percy politely.

"The bull trod on them" said Cuthbert.

"Where are the ducks?" tried Percy.

"The fox got them," nodded Cuthbert eagerly.

84

"And the bull?" queried Percy.

"Not sure," replied Cuthbert slowly "It may have left with the circus, it quite fancied the Hippo."

This went on for a while until they had exhausted all farm animals and even a particularly psychopathic weasel was unaccounted for. By this point, even Cuthbert was sensing a pattern.

Percy tried another tack, "Finances and takings?"

Cuthbert was nodding as if the spring in his neck had become loose and he rummaged around in an ancient oak cupboard which was notorious for not letting go of anything placed in its care. Eventually, he staggered backwards clutching an old strong-box which seemed to weigh a ton and dropped it onto the table with a crash. Dusting off his hands he made to go back and search for the key, but Percy stopped him with a wave of his hand.

Cuthbert gawped as Percy opened the lid and removed a wad of notes from inside.

"But, how, when, where?" spluttered Cuthbert.

Percy was dismissive, "Oh I ignored the lock and took the pins out of the hinges ages ago" he said laying out a bed of paper banknotes along the table top.

"Cuthbert," he sighed "not one of these is still legal tender, is that Cromwell on that one?"

Percy prompted a bemused Cuthbert on to the next subject with the word "Security?"

"Blind Pugh," replied Cuthbert confidently.

Percy hooked his thumbs into a pretend waistcoat and paced up and down in his best courtroom manner before saying, "So, the whole security detail will be a blind sheepdog that will only attack if the threat is behind it?"

Cuthbert nodded.

Percy continued, "So if the thief runs in front of security, the money has gone?" Cuthbert nodded slowly waiting for the catch.

Percy changed tack again, "And what about the undertaking business?" Now, this was somewhat of a puzzle, even Cuthbert had to admit. If there was such a thing as a dry spell in the internment trade, the Valley was the Sahara because people were simply refusing to die anywhere near him.

Cuthbert had thought he had overheard a rumour that people were changing their names and moving away as soon as they showed any symptoms, but he was assured that it was only a rumour, just before the man who spread it changed his name and moved away.

Both Cuthbert and Percy were now seeing how pointless this exercise was, especially as Percy knew that he would be running the whole show anyway, so he waved a hand across the table and asked "What about the others, what will they do?"

Cuthbert's glance took in all the empty cups awaiting the regular visitors and shrugged, "Somebody's got to sell tickets, I suppose," he said.

Marvin sat with his head in his hands and looked at Henry in despair, "Not another project in the Valley; how many disasters will it take before you all learn to crochet and settle down?"

Henry was quite offended; he squirmed on his borrowed chair and refused to answer.

The fact was that he had learned to crochet years ago amongst the war zones of the world. Things could be quite boring when you stayed well back from the front lines and an extra blanket never came amiss.

Marvin was still remembering the monument to fallen Local Authority figures which somehow sank through a mire of radioactive sludge and disappeared.

Then there was the Circus and the Baking Contest and the battles with Aunt Liza (Henry shuddered).

Marvin sighed in resignation and accepted that the least he could do was inform the surveyor and his gormless assistant and send the road gang out to examine the site, so that he could peruse the planning side of things. He was pretty sure that between the dreams of the Valley and the nightmare of the planning authority, he could put this to bed and forget all about it.

He smiled at Henry, "They were playing Bridge you say, are they any good?"

Henry glazed over for a moment before replying, "Let's put it this way, next time I go in I'm taking a sharp stick to teach them how to play *Poker*."

Chapter Twenty-Eight

Elspeth stood at the window of the Mandrake Arms and said, "I never thought I'd say this, but just look at poor old Percy."

The rest of the women gathered around, but the sight was too good to have a pane of glass between them, so they all went outside for a better view.

Percy was stamping in and out of the old ironmonger's shop and the trick of the reflection made it seem as if he was walking into a mirror and disappearing only to re-appear carrying boxes and then loading them onto a huge cart.

Somehow, it only seemed a minor point that the cart was being towed by a dinosaur, this was Percy after all.

"What's he doing?" asked several of the women at once.

"He's clearing out our tea-room ladies; it won't be long before we can move in now."

"Isn't anyone helping him?" asked Elspeth kindly.

"He doesn't trust anyone shrugged Margery, he thinks that if the mafia get their hands on all those fixtures and fittings, he'll have to buy them back."

Under the street in one of the tunnels, a mafia member paused from the chore of passing boxes along a line to say, "Percy will be furious when he has to buy all this stuff back from us."

Jasper slapped him on the back and replied, "He's stashing it in Cuthbert's barn at the other end and the rest of the team are spreading it out to show buyers from the next valley."

A snigger ran down the line.

* * *

Standing outside the Mandrake Arms in the sunshine, Avril built up her courage to ask the other women, "Why is he using a dinosaur instead of a horse?"

Geraldine sniggered, "Oh, that's his animatronic dinosaur, he calls her Annie and he's convinced that we'll let him make them for the exhibitions when the time comes."

Avril pressed on, "But isn't that a tractor underneath the dinosaur?" she asked.

"Yes," boomed Arkle, "Why, do you think he won't get the contract?"

Taking advantage of having an audience, Arkle began to barrack Percy. "Come on man, I can carry twice as much as that. Why don't you put a saddle on 'Tin-Can-Annie' and ride her back?" She paused for a moment to focus on a spherical red object rolling towards her before giving out a shriek and bolting down the street.

The red object wobbled to a stop on the cobbles with it's drawn on smiley face grinning at the spot where Arkle had been.

The rest of the women were used to Arkle suddenly having to jump a few fences, but Avril picked up the tomato and studied the evidence,

Arkle had been mocking Percy and the tomato had rolled from Percy's direction.

There was something going on and it could well make an award winning story.

But even as the conspiracy tales weaved through her imagination like dragons chasing their tails, a tiny but significantly influential part of her brain was rewriting it as "Local man drops home-grown tomato and causes one person stampede." She put her notebook away.

Elspeth was still watching Percy and she mused "Look at the way his little arms and legs are going, can you imagine his reaction if he had to do our kind of work?"

Margery snorted "Hah, I once insisted that Henry help out in the house and trusted him to make a bed. When I checked, there was a load of spare material on one side; he'd used the duvet cover as a pillow case."

Everyone laughed as the women's favourite sport of man-baiting began.

Geraldine joined in with, "They really are useless; the man who invented queuing would have failed, if we hadn't all got behind him."

This caused spasms of delight and left Percy none the wiser as he watched from across the street with eyes like slits.

Chapter Twenty-Nine

Cecil Carruthers, the surveyor, stared at Marvin Middlewick and tried to gauge whether the man was trying to develop a sense of humour and this was an experiment.

He turned to Winston, his assistant who was playing air-guitar with Marvin's coat stand and plucked the earplugs and dangly wires from him to get his attention.

"Did you hear that?" the surveyor spluttered, "another survey of the Valley, another journey into the jaws of the mafia and another ridiculous project involving Cuthbert and Percy."

"Wow, cool" said his assistant flicking his fringe to one side, "That's where the talking trees are."

And with that, he began to show withdrawal symptoms and quickly connected again to his music. He began shaking to some random destruction of a well known melody.

"Talking trees?" asked Marvin suspiciously.

The surveyor sighed, "the mafia disguised themselves as papier-mâché' tree trunks to keep an eye on us last time and my esteemed assistant is convinced that he discovered an enchanted forest."

Now it was Marvin's turn to sigh as he unrolled a plan of the Valley. "This time it's the 'old end' of the Valley they want to desecrate."

"Old end?" interrupted the surveyor, "How can it be a different age to the 'new end', I mean 'other end?" He corrected himself.

Marvin waved a hand dismissively, "I know," he said, "This bunch can be quite medieval at times, you've got the 'old end' of the Valley and you've got the 'real Valley folk,' apparently.

The surveyor gritted his teeth as he asked "Is there by any chance a 'sane bit' where I can pitch my tent this time?"

* * *

Percy was stretching his arms above his head and wriggling to ease his back as Cuthbert put a steaming cup in front of him at the kitchen table.

The others watched with interest and waited for him begin his 'man of the soil and fruits of thy labour' speech.

"This is how it feels," he began, "Up at dawn with the cock crow and laying down a weary head at dusk when all thy labours are done."

"How do *you* know?" asked Ronald mischievously.

Percy glared, before retorting "The Plumm's have always been at the forefront of the world's workload and when they're not working, they're creating, did you know that they were responsible for the Great Vegetable Exchange System in Northern Europe?

As his audience looked around helplessly, Percy wriggled to get comfortable. "It was because of us that the Swedes started to measure their gold in carrots," he said.

"Carats Percy, not carrots" interrupted Henry.

Percy exploded, "Typical," he snapped, "You hadn't heard of it until two minutes ago and now you're re-inventing it for yourself. That's what you privileged types do, you think you know everything and yet you don't know the price of a potato."

Henry looked around the table, "Alright gentlemen; let's set Percy straight, how much is a potato?"

The Captain grumbled, "Only blessed potatoes I saw were when we had to peel the things in the army, we didn't have to buy them."

Ronald shrugged, as a mercenary the locals had always cooked for him in exchange for 'fire-water.'

Cuthbert looked thoroughly puzzled, when he had owned pigs he had wrestled them to the ground and confiscated the potatoes, but now he just found them in the fields.

Henry was on the verge of giving up, but he came back with "All right then, how much is a pint of milk, you must know this one Cuthbert, you make the tea."

A barely controlled panic crossed behind Cuthbert's eyes as he tried to not glance towards the bottle of embalming fluid by the sugar bowl, but he was saved by Percy stomping off upstairs on a one-man austerity march.

Chapter Thirty

Margery had assembled her reluctant troops in the now empty ironmongers shop.

Elspeth was raring to go, but Avril was looking at the gentle drifts of dust as if an underground tomb was about to collapse on them.

As an archaeologist, Geraldine had been inside a collapsing tomb and even she was worried. The situation wasn't helped by the lack of electricity in the Valley and the unrecognisable items each of the ladies were holding.

Arkle stood there like a mountain of tweed smelling of horse and wondering what on Earth she was expected to do with some feathers on a stick.

Avril dipped a mop into a bucket of water and by swinging it around, promptly washed her own feet.

Elspeth was in her element climbing a ladder with various grades of duster tucked into her belt, "Come on girls," she cried "Start at the top and the dust will fall down to where we can sweep it outside."

Margery opened the doors at the front and the back of the shop in the hope that a through draught would help, but it just created a vortex in the middle of the floor and circulated the dust they already had.

Geraldine was delicately brushing around something she had found on the floor as if it was a precious artefact when Margery thoughtfully stopped her, "I wouldn't bother dear, I think it's one of Percy's mouldy sandwiches."

Arkle had decided that this delicate approach was pointless, so she began to shake the big wall cabinets displacing tons of dust and dislodging Elspeth from her ladder.

The conditions were so bad now that a canary in a coal mine wouldn't have survived, so they all gasped and spluttered outside where they were met by a man with a clip-board.

"Furniture delivery for some tea-room somewhere," He muttered, totally distracted by the sight of a dust-covered Arkle holding a stick with one feather left in it.

Margery asked quietly, "Where is it?"

91

"Where's what?" answered the delivery driver.

"The furniture" said Margery patiently.

"Over there," replied the man waving vaguely towards The Mandrake Arms.

Margery waited politely before she said, "I don't see any furniture."

Arkle added, "I don't see any van."

The man stared from one of them to the other and a vague memory began to surface; some time ago he had read an article in the Deliverer's Digest about a valley where strange things happened, vans and their loads disappeared and there were rampant hallucinations after which the victims never spoke of them again.

"They've gone?" He asked with a gulp,

"Oh yes," said the ladies in unison.

"How will I get home?" asked the driver, very aware that he was trembling, but so was the ground beneath him and everyone seemed to be shouting over an ever increasing noise.

"Oh, I'm sure Percy and Annie will give you a lift" said Margery with a smile."

The driver looked around slowly trying to stay calm amongst the noise and vibrations and he was suddenly faced with, a red-haired chap sat on a dinosaur. The driver fainted.

Margery looked down at the unconscious driver, shook her head and yelled, "Jasper."

Jasper almost joined them, but Constable Beeching pulled up beside the group and began his complicated contortions to get out of his car, so Jasper nipped into the new tea-room and hid amongst the dust.

Everyone waited until the officer had struggled upright and focused upon the prone figure. "Stand back," he shouted in his official voice "This is a crime scene, someone find me a piece of chalk.

The Captain huffed "chalk? You don't need to write it down, you nincompoop we all heard you."

The Constable glared and informed them that it was standard practice to draw a chalk outline around the body."

"Why? Margery asked mischievously. "If it's a body, it won't be going anywhere."

Percy simply had to join in with, "Well, if it escapes, at least you'll know where it's been."

Beeching stopped trying to bend far enough for his chalk to reach the ground and pointed at Percy, "I thought I told you to get a licence for that thing?"

Percy put his hands over the places where dinosaur's ears would be if they had any and the head swung menacingly towards the constable.

Percy countered with, "It doesn't need one because it's attached to the tractor and that makes it a trailer."

The Officer spluttered, "That's not a trailer, trailers go behind."

Percy replied smugly, "Well, that's where the tail is."

Whilst all this had been going on, Margery had helped the 'body' to his feet and taken him across the road to the bar for a drink.

Ronald had been busy with the chalk. "Look," said Ronald pointing dramatically at the outlines on the floor, "Those outlines have been getting smaller, you almost caught Shrinking Malcolm."

Constable Beeching stared. The outlines were the perfect shape of where the body had been, but there where several decreasing sizes as the body had indeed shrunk.

"Shrinking Malcolm?" spluttered the officer "Whose he?"

Henry took up his cue by sucking air through his teeth and explaining, "When I was a reporter, the whole of the police force was looking for Shrinking Malcolm. He could get in anywhere, grab the money and jewels and then get out again through the smallest gaps. That's how he got his name."

Elspeth could see the interest in the Constable's eyes, so she offered, "He must be worth a fortune by now."

Henry did an imitation of Percy's anti-climactic shoulder slump and sighed, "Unfortunately not, most of his ill-gotten gains were left at the next obstruction. That's how the police deduced that he could shrink, but the jewels wouldn't, so he only got away with paper money and small coins.

You almost caught a legend and went down in police history there Beeching."

The officer gasped and stared around wildly trying to find the fugitive. He was staring down into the smallest chalk outline in case the crook was playing shrunken possum when he heard a scuffle and a sneeze. "Stand back," his said grabbing a stick with a feather on it from Arkle, looking at it in amazement and accepting a brush from Elspeth.

"This is not a job for Joe Public," he announced before charging into the new tea-rooms.

"Not a job for PC Plonker either at a guess," giggled Percy as they all wandered across the road together.

Jasper was happily sat at the bar with his orange juice and everyone settled down to await developments.

Elspeth was giving a running commentary from the window and she was really impressed, "The dust is flying out and every time there's a pile he comes out and beats it with the brush handle."

Eventually, when the dust had settled (so to speak), the Constable came gasping into the bar; he picked up Percy's pint and downed it in one go before anyone could explain that Percy had just drained the spillage trays and was on his way to the drains with it.

The Constable had swept the tea-room with his brush and now he swept the bar room with his eyes; there was something not right he thought, there were too many people here.

Percy had sat down with Cuthbert, Henry and the Captain and Ronald was chatting to someone with his back to the officer.

All the women were present and correct, but his trained antenna was twitching. Walking over to the bar, he whispered to Ronald "Who's that you're talking to then?"

Ronald didn't miss a beat and he replied, "It's Whistle, he lowers his hood in company you know."

The Constable looked closer, "Doesn't look like Whistle" he pointed out.

"How do you know?" asked Ronald.

Constable Beeching thought about all the times he had met Whistle and his hood had always been up, so he had to admit that Ronald had a point.

Next, he focused on a person sat at the bar with a drink, he was smaller than everyone else who wasn't Percy, so it seemed a good place to start. He eased into place beside the suspect and began his interrogation with "All right Shrinking Malcolm, the games up and you're coming with me."

Jasper turned to him and replied "Not a chance mate, I was always told never to go off with strange men."

The Constable was appalled, "I'm not a strange man; I'm an officer of the law."

Jasper watched as one of the mafia appeared briefly behind the officer and then signalled with a thumbs-up sign.

Jasper continued, "Well from here you look like a great dusty lump who's just handcuffed himself to his chair."

Beeching jumped to his feet taking the bar stool with him and promptly fell sideways, skittling the other stools as he went.

This gave Jasper the chance to finish his drink and wander away with a casual wave.

The women all fussed around Beeching and dusted him down as he tried to impress them with "Did you see that?

I had Shrinking Malcolm and he shrank right out of my grip. Don't worry ladies; you'll be safe with me." When everything had calmed down again, Margery introduced Beeching to the stranded van driver and asked whether he could give him a lift out of the Valley.

The Officer begrudgingly agreed to clear some empty pizza boxes out and make room for him and as they left the Mandrake Arms, Henry heard Beeching ask his passenger for his name. "Little," came the reply "Malcolm Little."

Chapter Thirty-One

The ladies stood in the old ironmongers shop and gasped.

Constable Beeching had done an amazing job, even Elspeth was impressed.

The mahogany and glass counters could be turned and re-used to display cakes and the taller wall units could be filled with interesting bric-a-brac as soon as Jasper and his mafia returned all the stock they had stolen from the next bring and buy sale.

* * *

Geraldine sat thoughtfully in the Museum office and wondered if these developments were the best thing for her.

She had carved out a niche for herself here and her sudden rages only seemed to relate to Percy, so that was an improvement.

The thing was that this was her kingdom; no-one with a hyphenated name came along to check her work and steal all the best bits and there was no-one to question her opinion.

She had found that really irritating when some old duffer stood up mid-lecture and started to correct her, just because he looked ancient didn't mean that he had *been there.*

Geraldine forced herself to calm down and she rummaged in a drawer for her pills not knowing that the mafia had found them weeks ago and kept topping them up with coloured sweets.

She had momentarily wondered why they were lasting so long, but had put it down to self-discipline.

It wouldn't be easy to stop the project because everyone was so keen to make it work, but an influx of beard-sprouting sandal wearers would not be in her best interests.

Geraldine smiled thinly, they were all relying upon her specialist knowledge and the Valley had an amazing capacity for never quite moving forward, all she had to do was slowly downplay her enthusiasm and make sure that no more footprints or artefacts came to light.

* * *

The Captain had reached new heights in the eye-brow raising stakes when he stared at Cuthbert and demanded, "What caves, what paintings?"

Cuthbert shrugged, they knew about the footprints, it wasn't his fault that they hadn't gone far enough down the tunnels afterwards.

Arkle had moved the counter across the floor to where it would act as a barrier between the staff and the mugs that paid them and in doing so she revealed a trapdoor in the floor.

Climbing down a ladder and flicking a switch, Elspeth was heard to say "Oooh, is that another load of footprints?"

* * *

Geraldine was making her way down the High Street to the Mandrake Arms to begin her campaign of disillusionment when the women burst out of the new tea-shop and the men ran out of the pub.

The Archaeologist found herself to be the centre of attention as the women gabbled about "more footprints in the basement," and the men contributed "huge caves with wall paintings."

"Oh good grief," muttered Geraldine.

Chapter Thirty-Two

Obviously, Ronald was in charge of the expedition, but Cuthbert had been roped in as a reluctant guide, as he was the only one who knew where the cave was, otherwise he would have been tending to the animals he didn't have and reading Farmer's Weekly or counting his plots and reading Undertaker's Times.

Either way, the kettle would have been on and he would be sat in peace.

Ronald was fully kitted out with an assault suit and head torch as was his brother Henry.

The Captain was sulking because there wasn't one for him.

Percy was sulking because Ronald had ticked off on his fingers the amount of times Percy had blown him up when trusted with one and now he had run out of fingers.

Cuthbert was sulking because this was his life all over. He felt as if he was on the board during a game of chess and all the pieces knew where to move to, but he was in the way and at the end of it all. Even if his team won, somehow his name wouldn't be on the cup.

At the edge of the hole where Percy had fallen in, they all waited whilst Ronald tied a rope around Cuthbert's waist and then turned to tie it around Percy.

Satisfied that his biggest liabilities couldn't wander off, he began his speech, "Gentlemen, this could be a dangerous endeavour but you are a professional team and I expect your utmost endeavours."

Cuthbert's team all looked at each other, this was odd; Ronald's lips were moving but the words and voice were someone else's, in fact it sounded like Marvin.

Peering behind a bush, Henry gave a cheerful wave and invited Marvin, the Drains Inspector and his team to join them.

The drains team tried to hide their envy when they saw Ronald and Henry in tactical overalls and wearing head torches, but curiosity really got the better of them when they saw Cuthbert and Percy roped together.

"Hurr, hurr, is it a firing squad Ronald?

Somebody will hear the shots," commented one lung Louie.

"What's going on?" asked Marvin catching up before Ronald could congratulate Louie on a change of plan, going back for some ammunition and carrying it out.

"What are you lot doing here?" Henry gently steered Marvin away from the hole and they placated each other and even decided that they could explore together.

Eventually, they dropped down into the hole one by one like paratroopers exiting a plane, Cuthbert had been put in front as the guide and Buster was the last man.

Cuthbert had been issued with a torch which seemed to be determined to imitate a flickering candle, so that everyone's shadows leapt about like a frenetic ballet dance.

"Stand still Cuthbert," hissed Ronald "If the bulb is loose, give the thing a shake."

Cuthbert sighed, here he was again put in a position of responsibility and knowing full well whose responsibility it would be when it went wrong. Shaking the torch in darkness seemed completely pointless because Cuthbert couldn't see where it went when it slipped out of his hand, but a dull thud and a groan from Ronald gave him some idea.

"Quick," shouted Percy "Grab his head torch and follow me."

Cuthbert grabbed the torch and looked around for Percy, but it was of course dark. The first Cuthbert knew of Percy's whereabouts was when the rope tightened and he was pulled along rapidly.

The two friends ran as fast as they could, but with Percy thumping into everything in the dark, it really slowed them down.

Eventually, even Percy suspected that he was concussed and had to sit down.

"If only you had grabbed the head torch," moaned Percy.

"Which, this one?" asked Cuthbert, switching it on and illuminating a huge cave covered in crude paintings of animals.

Percy stared, it was like being in a huge cartoon, and he almost expected roadrunner to be in there somewhere.

Henry and the road gang had managed to catch up and Buster came in last, supporting Ronald who was muttering incomprehensibly and yet managing to make it sound murderous at the same time.

Everyone now stood and gaped.

Marvin and Henry exchanged looks which prompted Henry to ask "Have you ever seen anything like this before?"

Marvin nodded, as C.L.O.S.E.D. or Cultural Liaison Officer Supervising Excavations and Digging, he had attended seminars all over the world at taxpayer's expense and whilst Doreeen had tested sun-loungers for a fortnight, he had escaped into the caves.

"The finest ones are in France," he breathed "They are so old and delicate that the public are now banned because even the breath of a group of people can ruin them."

A moment passed and a series of thuds caused him to add, "For goodness sake, start breathing again you dozy lot, this cave is huge and it should be all right for some years yet."

Various torches were shining in different directions and Ronald seemed to be edging closer to Cuthbert and clutching what looked like a rock-hammer.

"What's that?" exclaimed Buster nervously pointing upwards to where a rotating light seemed to getting closer and it was accompanied by a swishing sound. It looked as if someone was lowering the top of a lighthouse down towards them.

Gradually, they could make out a voice, it was Geraldine lowering herself down by rappelling and she was shouting to someone above, "Oh, this amazing, it's wonderful, it's unique. Keep the rope tight Ar.." "Ar..?" came a growl from above.

Geraldine pulled her wits together and quickly added "Are you seeing this?"

Arkle growled again and said, "Of course I'm not, I'm up here and you're down there."

Geraldine gave a sigh of relief; she could never hope to keep this a secret, so it was best if no-one else saw it. Concentrating on landing squarely and unfastening her quick-release gear, she was startled when Percy asked "watcha doing?"

Geraldine's heart lurched, she was surrounded by potential witnesses to the greatest secret of all time, she momentarily considered pulling sharply on the rope and bringing Arkle through the hole and the ceiling down at the same time, but that would turn the cave into a quarry and everyone would see it. Besides, she'd tried to eliminate some of these twerps before and they all had charmed lives.

This was obviously a time for subtlety, so she began with "I'm surprised to see you lot this close to the radiation."

"Radiation?" gasped Henry, adjusting the collar on his tactical suit and breathing through the neck.

"Quick Ronald, protect yourself," he cried.

Ronald gave an embarrassed shrug before saying, "Ah, about that Henry, we don't have any filters in the suits, the mafia nicked them; they thought they were tea bags."

Marvin was flapping his arms and looking at Geraldine in horror, "Why would there be radiation down here? My whole team is at risk."

The drains inspector and his men huddled together, the word team didn't always mean much to them, but *risk* certainly did.

Geraldine paused for effect, before saying "Oh it's the old paint, over all those years the pigment has reacted to the oxide in the rocks and produced radioactivity, why do you think we use little brushes on everything we find before we handle it?"

Pausing again, she looked from one face to the other and added "We brush the radiation off first."

Marvin found himself surrounded by the Drains Inspector and his team, the questions being thrown at him varied from "Did you know about this?" to "What do I tell my Mum?" and "Are we on overtime?"

Henry wasn't convinced, he'd seen the cave paintings abroad as well and there had been no mention of radiation. "What about Howard Carter?" he asked, "He never mentioned it when he opened Tutankhamen's tomb; he just said, 'I see wonderful things."

Geraldine thought quickly, "He never mentioned that everything was glowing green either did he, why do you think he let the locals carry everything outside?"

On top of the hill above the cave, Arkle secured the rope to a tree and joined Margery Avril and Elspeth on the gingham tablecloth where their picnic was laid out.

After quietly enjoying a sandwich, Margery asked "Does anyone think Geraldine is acting strangely?"

"How would we tell?" asked Arkle, wondering why no-one made a decent sized sandwich these days.

Margery nodded towards Avril and replied "She has the perfect method to get her findings out to the world, Avril here has all the contacts and yet she hasn't even photographed the footprints yet. Do you think she's going off the idea of the theme park?"

"I hope not, "spluttered Elspeth "I've just borrowed a pig-feeder from Cuthbert to mix my Victoria sponge in ready for when the crowds start."

Margery tried to push that image away as she raised her voice and said "Jasper, code one, Geraldine."

A nearby bush stood to attention and after a series of hand signals; another bush detached itself and began moving downhill.

The men were making their way back down the tunnel and into the river bed, there were footprints all the way into the cave, but they didn't seem to come back out.

Percy pointed this out loudly and one-lung Louie and swivelling Simon moved closer together.

They had also recognised the 'slap-slap' sound of Percy's wellies as they walked and it brought back memories, none of them good.

Henry and Marvin had automatically assumed a position of shared authority and they were leading the orderly exit. "Isn't this going to bring all sorts of preservation headaches and ownership wrangles?" asked Henry.

Marvin hesitated, because he had already been considering just how much his workload would increase and he already knew that whatever decisions he made, there would be pitchfork wielding villagers at his office window.

"I've been thinking the same thing," he muttered so that only Henry could hear. "We don't even *know* who owns the Valley because nobody *wants* it."

Henry remembered the disputes over ownership when Percy thought he had sold the Valley to The Great Dragon Dropping only to find that he had given it away.

"It turned out at that time that Cuthbert owned most of it because people who died left him a piece of land in lieu of funeral expenses."

Marvin snorted, "Half the time, it turned out that the piece they had left him was the piece they were buried in and anyway, this is the 'old end of the Valley,' so unless those wall paintings are land deeds and indentures we would have been better off not finding them."

Henry could see that things were not going to be clear cut and he was starting to have reservations.

This was all having a strange effect on Avril too. As the local journalist, she had been so close to so many scoops in this Valley, but at the last moment, the walls seemed to close in and the news wasn't allowed out, why should this be any different?

She vaguely listened to the chatter of her friends Arkle, Margery and Elspeth as they enjoyed their picnic, flipped open her notebook and stared at the empty pages in the same way that Cuthbert used to stare at the shiny spiral.

She caught herself smiling and wondered whether she really wanted any of it to change.

Margery noticed the smile and nodded knowingly as Elspeth squeezed her hand.

Ronald had been left with a lump on his head so that his head torch was pointing off at an awkward angle; it was a good job that he always carried a spare.

A strange thought suddenly came to him, he seemed to have learned more about guerrilla tactics since he'd known Cuthbert and Percy than he had in all his years as a mercenary and of course he refused to accept defeat against the mafia because they were 'just kids.'

He plodded on, deep in thought with his head twisted to compensate for the errant beam of light as the lump on his head throbbed in time with his footsteps.

Stumbling over yet another set of indented dinosaur footprints, he sighed; it was going to change the Valley beyond recognition. An old saying came to him "you don't know what you've got 'till it's gone, of course the military version was "you don't know what you've got till it's shot."

Perhaps he could go back to being a mercenary, he could contact his old comrade Hans who had been eaten by lions three times, and insurance payouts were always handy when the jobs dried up.

He sighed again, being a soldier was a young man's game, he remembered wading through a swamp holding his rifle above his head and feeling it get heavier and heavier.

It wasn't until he reached the firmer ground that he discovered two alligators, one hanging from each end of it. Adjusting his head torch to stop it chafing on the bump, he also remembered why he had left the army and become a 'soldier of fortune.'

Their new commander had appeared to prepare them for the upcoming battle and after a rousing speech full of, "Some will lose limbs and some will lose their lives, but I remain undaunted by any of this."

"Why is that boss?" asked Ronald. "Because I'm not going," said the officer flatly and walked away, and so did Ronald.

Now Arkle wasn't especially tuned in to the feelings of humans; if they had four legs and a tail she would have been an expert, but as it was, they insisted on thinking and making decisions, so it was all very confusing, but she could recognise change when she saw it.

The thought of losing her beloved steeple-chasing and having to look out for people getting in the way brought complications, and Arkle didn't like complications, her idea of resolving a situation was by giving Percy a thump, it was like adding a full stop to the day.

Chapter Thirty-Three

The atmosphere around Cuthbert's table was a strange one, but that was probably because the road gang had joined them and the heat from the cooking range was sucking out the vapours from several weeks of digging, rodding and plunging.

Percy's wellies were trying hard to compete as well.

Henry opened the debate, whilst trying to talk with his mouth closed, but he gave up and ushered everyone outside where they perched on various pieces of rusting sculpture posing as farm machinery.

"This project is bigger than anything we imagined," Henry began, "Those cave paintings alone will bring the world to our doorstep and Geraldine has found more footprints in the cellar of the old Ironmonger's shop, they must be everywhere just below the soil."

The women had gradually been joining the men and carefully staying downwind of the road gang and Geraldine confirmed that she had indeed found more.

"So what?" asked Margery, "That will bring customers to the tea-room *and* to The Mandrake Arms."

Geraldine shuffled her feet and bit her bottom lip, "Margery" she said slowly, "The footprints are heading straight towards The Mandrake Arms."

Margery looked from face to face and burst out laughing, "Oh for goodness sake," she spluttered "Anyone would think they were still alive and we were all doomed."

Now it was Henry's turn to look uncomfortable, he turned to Marvin and nodded.

Marvin took a deep breath and explained, "If this news gets out, the whole Valley will probably be hit by a preservation order and closed off for an archaeological dig."

Margery rubbed her hands together, but found herself wondering why she was the only one seeing the bright side. "Well, that's even more customers then."

There was still no sign of enthusiasm, it was like having your execution order read out in a foreign language, but you didn't mind because everyone was smiling.

Henry sat her down gently and Jasper brought her a cup of Cuthbert's tea, but by the time he reached her, the contents had eaten through the cup and the handle had dropped off.

Henry patted the back of his wife's hand and said carefully "Darling, they will probably demolish the Ironmongers shop to reveal the footprints properly, so that's the tearoom gone."

Margery took it well and bounced back with, "Back to square one then, the tearoom will be in the Mandrake Arms."

Jasper shook his head and reminded her that "the footprints are heading right for The Mandrake Arms, they'll flatten that too."

Margery looked around wildly and her eyes settled on Marvin, "Is this true?"

Marvin had always had a soft spot for 'that Margery,' but he couldn't think of a way to make any of it seem like good news. "I'm afraid so, once the archaeologists start,"

He turned to Geraldine who nodded in confirmation; "They'll cordon off the whole Valley so that work will be uninterrupted by anyone, it could take years."

The sombre mood spread amongst them all like ink on blotting paper, the only people unaffected were Cuthbert and Percy because they weren't there.

Cuthbert and Percy had gone outside with everyone else, but Percy had eased Cuthbert towards the barn because "That bunch are going to rabbit away for hours and we'll end up selling tickets," so they didn't hear any of the discussion, but Percy was in full invention mode anyway, the greasy rag had appeared in his top pocket and a retractable tape measure was being convinced that it really should stay out instead of rocketing back in and rapping Percy's knuckles.

Nothing in this building should have been a mystery to Cuthbert as he owned it and he had spent his whole life here, but the complication was that Percy was always dismantling the stuff he recognised and building it into something he didn't, so he found it very hard to keep up.

That pair of wings propped up in the corner for instance, where had they come from?

Very shortly, Cuthbert was engaged in man-handling the wings up to the barn roof where Percy had rigged up a giant catapult in the hayloft. The wings were spread and Percy tinkered here and there placing square sheets of paper into a special holder underneath the contraption.

Standing back and giving his forehead a tribal smear of engineering grease, he pulled a lever and Cuthbert dived flat to avoid joining the launch.

Outside, it was generally being agreed that although at long last the Valley had this viable money earning project and a genuine place on the tourist map, it was not going to benefit the inhabitants at all. It was becoming more and more obvious that this news *must not leak out*.

At that moment the sky darkened and something dreadful whirred overhead scattering what looked like shedding feathers behind it.

Everyone ran for cover, except Jasper who was made of sterner stuff and as he controlled the airspace rents in the Valley, he soon spotted Percy jumping up and down on the barn roof. "What have you done now you nitwit?" shouted Ronald picking up a sheet of paper dropped by the apparition zooming out of the valley.

"That's Terry Dactyl, that is," shouted Percy in reply, "Get ready for business."

Ronald looked at the 'flyer' in his hand and blanched. He handed it wordlessly to Henry who read out "**Grand opening gala-The Valley of the Dinosaurs-huge cave where you can try painting by numbers-meet Annie Matronic and her innovative creator, Percy Plumm.**"

The crowd of locals moved as one organism, it steered around obstacles and coalesced again as it headed towards the barn with everyone united by a single purpose.

"Ooops," said Percy.

Chapter Thirty-Four

That evening in the bar, everyone seemed to have calmed down, so after checking through the windows, Percy sauntered in and took his place at a table. "Evening chaps," he said, his hand groping in mid-air at the point where his pint should have been.

As a gardener, he had always had a keen sense of the changing seasons and the sudden frostiness around him gave him a familiar feeling, "It's a trap" he muttered.

Everyone had something to say about Percy, none of it was quiet, none of it was kind and none of it was complimentary.

During a desperately needed breathing space, Percy wailed, "How was I supposed to know? The last I heard we were opening up Plumm's Animatronics Wonderland and you lot were selling tickets."

This set everyone off again and Percy slumped in his seat until the storm had washed over him, it could take a while, especially without a pint.

* * *

The next day brought PC Beeching hammering on Margery's door and trying to arrest someone for littering.

Margery was in no mood for him, so she promptly sent him to Percy's door, which was in fact Cuthbert's door, which was an awful lot for the poor man to take in and by the time he collapsed at the kitchen table, he was even distracted enough to accept a cup of tea.

"Littering," he gasped at Percy who sat watching him warily before answering, "I don't have a dog."

"What's a dog got to do with it?" wheezed the PC.

"He's right," added Cuthbert helpfully, "we don't have a dog, but perhaps we should, every farm should have a sheepdog."

But we don't have any sheep," Percy reminded him.

Cuthbert brightened, "That's right; we don't have any sheep, so we don't have a dog, so it can't have been Percy."

The officer looked from one to the other trying to figure out why his superior training and intellect wasn't winning the day.

"For the last time, what's a dog got to do with it?" Beeching demanded.

"Percy sighed "If we don't have a dog, it won't have had puppies, so we can't have been littering now can we?" He pointed out quite reasonably.

PC Beeching exploded, "Not that sort of litter, this sort of litter," he shouted, pulling a handful of Percy's flyers out of his pocket and causing them to scatter everywhere.

"You can't do that," scalded Percy "That's littering, that is." T

The officer made a visible effort to stay calm as he stabbed a finger at a name on the flyer, "Is that your name?" he hissed. "Hugh Cave?

No, definitely not" said Percy causing the Constable to look closer and move his finger from Huge Cave to Percy Plumm.

"Oh yes." said Percy happily, but Annie Matronic is the ring leader, it's her you need to talk to or the distributor Terry Dactyl."

The constable was writing furiously just as the Captain and Henry came in, the Captain had been unsettled by recent developments and he was in a strange mood. "Don't you stand when a superior officer enters the room?" he snapped.

Beeching jumped to his feet scattering more paper all over the floor and stood to attention whilst his flab rippled and caught up with the sudden movement.

The Captain snatched one of the sheets of paper up and thrust it in front of Beeching, "So it's you who's scattering this stuff everywhere is it my lad?"

Somehow, every inch of him seemed to bristle and the Constable tried desperately to remember who his superior officer should be, but they were so efficient at avoiding him that he was at a loss.

"At ease man" snapped the Captain tiring of the game and taking a seat.

Then began the laborious process of informing the Constable of all the recent developments and making him see why it was in everyone's interests to keep it quiet. It wasn't until they pointed out that he would be transferred to somewhere where people could see him that he began to panic.

Chapter Thirty-Five

Margery and the ladies were gathered in The Mandrake Arms grieving for the gingham paradise they were about to forfeit, but customers wouldn't come without any attractions, but the attractions would ruin the valley.

Just at that moment, a squealing of tyres outside announced the arrival of a bus and a meaningful glance at the pot plant in the corner dispatched Jasper through the tunnels to Cuthbert's farm where the men had reduced Constable Beeching to a gibbering wreck at the thought of genuine police work and they were busy congratulating themselves that the dinosaur problem had solved itself by them simply ignoring it.

Jasper burst in through a sliding panel that no-one had noticed before and he simply started throwing people into the tunnel shouting "Code red, priority one, Mandrake Arms, now."

Beeching had landed first so everyone else bounced and rolled off him.

Unfortunately, this was not the disciplined mafia that Jasper was used to and they all stood milling about in the dark muttering things like "What? Where? Whom?"

Jasper sighed before calling down into the darkness, "A bus full of bearded men in sandals has come into the Valley, move it."

Now they all knew that nothing good ever came from sandals or beards, so this was serious and they all dashed back to the sliding panel, but Jasper's sense of mischief had got the better of him and he had stolen the ladder, so it was back to ricocheting off the walls shouting "Cuthbert, where are the candles?"

Jasper sat on the edge of the doorway with his legs dangling into the tunnel enjoying the chaos until he remembered that Margery had sent him and he lowered the ladder again.

By the time the men reached the pub, the ladies had served non-alcoholic fruit drinks to their visitors and they were all watching each other warily.

The person who seemed to be the leader; gave a sigh of relief when he saw the men and he promptly shook Henry's hand and introduced himself as Professor North, Chief Archaeologist.

It was obvious that the only women he was comfortable around were mummies.

He then turned and introduced Professor South who also shook hands.

"I say," exclaimed the Captain "That's clever, have you already allocated search zones?"

The visitor looked puzzled, "Oh no," he replied "Professor East is in charge of that."

Another visitor stepped forward and shook hands all round.

Margery's voice was icy as she asked, "Do you have any intention of introducing your *female* team members then or have your manners gone west?"

A female voice giggled, "Oh, very good, I like that one."

Professor North looked at the women as if he was seeing them for the first time and waved a hand dismissively, "Oh, we've brought some assistants with us" he said as Margery clenched her fists and Henry stepped between them.

In an attempt to break the tension, Henry asked, "So, what can we do for you gentlemen, we weren't expecting visitors."

The Professor shrugged and replied "We're the vanguard; as soon as we've ascertained the validity of these leaflets; we will close the Valley and begin several digs at once." He paused before continuing, "Now, if you can direct me to the local archaeologist?"

The crowd parted like The Red Sea and there stood Percy, hat askew from running, ginger hair bursting out from beneath his hat and leaflets tucked into his turned-down wellies.

"Oh," said the Professor looking him up and down, you must be Gerald Dean; we have obviously disturbed you during a dig, I really must congratulate you on these finds of yours."

It was too much for Geraldine and she stepped forward only to find Margery's hand on her arm in a vice-like grip, "Don't say a word," she hissed; "If anyone can send this bunch running, it's Percy."

Geraldine was appalled, "You are trusting the future of the Valley to Percy *again*?"

Percy, for his part began by resenting the assumption that he could save the day, but when he thought about it, the others were only going to be a bunch of ticket sellers anyway, and besides, those female assistants were paying him an awful lot of attention.

Professor North was addressing him "So, Mr Dean, or may I call you Gerald?"

Percy nodded as he tried to decide between the love of his life and his soul mate who were eagerly soaking up his wisdom.

The Professor continued "What is the optimum depth for the best results in the Valley?" he was asking.

Percy blushed as one of the girls winked at him and he spluttered, "Oh, about a foot down generally."

The Professors were surprised, "That seems shallow for artefacts" said one and Percy realised his error, "Oh, that's for rhubarb," he said before adding "The footprints are much deeper."

"*Footprints?*" echoed the archaeological team and Geraldine took the opportunity to give Margery a look, whistle tunelessly and walk away.

Percy had dashed into the bar, but they had followed him and he found himself at the centre of a maelstrom of beards, sandals and questions.

All the Professors were asking questions he wasn't supposed to answer and none of the women had asked him out yet, this wasn't going to plan at all.

The rest of the Valley's population was gathered at the other end of the bar and as much as they were enjoying Percy's discomfort, they knew that he would crack eventually, so Ronald came up with a plan which involved sending Cuthbert back through the tunnels to his farm and the mafia helping him to create a séance-type scenario to lead everyone off the scent.

After giving Cuthbert time to get back home, the Captain approached Percy's tormentors and coughed to get their attention, "Excuse me chaps, but are you the scientific and unimaginative type of archaeologists or have you been inducted into the mysteries?"

Percy gabbled helplessly, "They're amateurs they don't even brush the radioactivity off with that little brush."

The Captain waved him to silence and repeated the question, the majority of the visitors looked at him blankly but Professors' North and South shuffled uncomfortably and asked, "What do you mean?"

The Captain nodded wisely and said, "I have seen things that you wouldn't believe, but they have left death and destruction behind them and I have heard music the like of which we can never recreate. You have entered the tombs of Egypt?" he asked.

The Professors nodded mutely, so the Captain said enigmatically "Then you know, don't you." He then beckoned them to follow him through a panel in the bar room wall and they all walked in single file through a long tunnel.

Along the route, voices could be heard to whisper, "Look, masons' marks in the stonework and "Look, original tool marks" and, "Where is the old fool taking us?"

The Captain had led the way with a paraffin lamp and someone at the back had another one, but when they reached a large opening they both plunged the scene into darkness.

The Captain announced, "We will climb this ladder in silence and take a seat in silence, anyone who cannot handle this must go back now.

There was a scuffling sound as several people took him up on the opportunity and scuttled away in the darkness.

Entering Cuthbert's kitchen through the trapdoor, they were met by the heat and glow of the kitchen range in an otherwise darkened room, and sat at the end of the long table illuminated by the flickering shades of heat was Cuthbert.

Just plain old uncomplicated Cuthbert, but Jasper had very cleverly torn a metal spiral from the top of Avril's notebook and laid it before him and Cuthbert's eyes were rolling as he followed the spiral in one direction and then back in the other when he reached the end.

Sensing that everyone who dared to stay had stayed, the Captain asked in a neutral voice. "Are you the keeper of the secrets?"

There was a moment's silence when Ronald eased a bit closer, in case he needed to do some prompting, but Cuthbert answered, "Yes, I am."

Professors' North and South gasped in unison, they had seen mystics before in far off lands and they leaned forward.

One of them asked, "Do you know of any footprints?"

Henry gasped, he hadn't expected Cuthbert to have to handle this question, but he relaxed when the answer came.

"This valley is as old as time, those who have walked it have faded even from their own memories."

The Professor persisted, "But are there footprints?"

Cuthbert sighed and the kitchen range dribbled ash as if a volcano was preparing to blow. "Recent ones or from before the rocks were hard?" he asked.

The Professor jumped to his feet and Henry held his head in his hands. Why did it always come down to the two resident clowns to get them out of trouble?

The Professor was waving his arms about in excitement, "Yes, yes, before the rocks were hard that's when the dinosaurs would have trodden in the mud and the solid rock would preserve it for us, can we see them?"

Cuthbert let the tension reach breaking point before saying, "What the ground gives, the water takes away. What was mud became slime and washed into the sea."

Professor North slumped into a chair desperately disappointed as Cuthbert stopped watching the spiral and his head slumped.

Henry ushered the visitors out and pointed them down the road to the village, then he went back and thumped Cuthbert on the back, "Brilliant," he cried, "Well done Cuthbert, no-one could have done it better."

Cuthbert woke up startled at all the fuss and asked "Are they here yet?"

Chapter Thirty-Six

Percy had stayed behind with the ladies, as soon as any of them realised that their fate was in Cuthbert's hands, they had known they were doomed.

When the Professors and their assistants trudged into the bar as if they had the pyramids on their shoulders and started to order alcohol, the whole Valley began to sense a reprieve, so Margery turned on the charm and served them personally, "What will it be gents and ladies?" she asked brightly in her best imagined barmaid's manner which had Belinda sulking instantly.

Professor North sighed and whispered, "Something small and strong and keep it coming."

"There's not enough of Percy to go round, but I'll put something in a glass for you" she quipped, but the only reaction was for Percy to join Belinda in her sulk.

The men began to file back in from various panels in walls and trapdoors to the cellar, but Cuthbert had stayed at home and out of sight which was just as well because he had no idea what had just happened.

Henry sat up as the road gang entered, placed their order and then thoughtfully went to sit outside, before Margery could throw them and their room-clearing miasma out.

Marvin and the drains inspector joined Henry at his table and the conversation began to flow. "What brings you back into the Valley?" he asked Marvin.

Marvin gave the archaeologists a sour look and hissed, "We've been told to prepare the ground for all those digs this bunch have scheduled," and he took a long swig of his pint which was a sure sign of tension.

Henry laid a hand on his shoulder and confided, "Don't worry; it's been taken care of."

At that moment, Professor North sat up straight and fixed Percy with a stare which confirmed that he still thought that he was addressing a colleague and asked, "Where did this rumour start and who is this Percy Plumm who signed the leaflets?"

"What leaflets?" asked Percy desperately.

115

The Professor leant forward and plucked a leaflet from Percy's welly, "This one" he said.

Percy had learnt very little from being associated with Cuthbert, but now he tried one of his friend's most trusted tactics, he stayed quiet and stared.

Not to be put off, the Professor insisted, "You are Gerald Dean the resident archaeologist and an expert in these things, how did it all start?"

The locals groaned loudly, not only had this man referred to Percy as an *expert,* but he had also asked him to *start talking.*

Everyone who was aware of the possible consequences of these actions, held their breath.

"Well," said Percy nodding to acknowledge a pint from the professor, "It all began with a walk in the woods."

Margery looked around in panic for something heavy to hit him with, Ronald reached for a weapon and Henry prepared to have a very distracting heart attack.

Percy noticed that the female assistants were now sat at his feet and gazing at him rapturously, until he swung his little legs and they subtly moved away from his wellies.

He looked around and realised that this was the biggest crowd he had commanded for a long time, so he began.

"Did I tell you about my ancestor creating the Egyptian police force identity unit? It was referred to as the C.I.D. after Cheop's Investigative Department."

"What, recently?" asked Henry rather stupidly considering all his experiences of Percy.

"No," sneered Percy "Back in the days of the Pharaohs when all the treasures were being stolen from the tombs."

The Archaeologists gasped, but Ronald came in at this with "Yes you did and by the sounds of it, your mob was the one stealing the stuff with funny heads on and pretending to be Gods."

He sat back contentedly, expecting Percy to retire defeated, but Percy was in full flow, with an audience like Cuthbert (who had joined them without anyone noticing him yet), Henry, Ronald and the Captain and all these outsiders, it was a chance too good to miss.

"As soon as a report came in of nefarious activity..."

"They arrested all the Nefars?" suggested Cuthbert eagerly.

"They set the Sphinx on them?" enquired Ronald laconically.

116

"They suspended all pyramid selling?" asked Henry straight faced.

"Three strikes and you're out eh?

This would be the last Nile in their coffin," added the Captain.

The Archaeologists gasped again, how on earth had their colleague survived all this mocking negativity? He was obviously a man to be reckoned with.

Percy looked from one to the other and tried to clear his mind, this barracking didn't usually bother him, but now he had professionals to impress, so ignoring everyone he continued. "Imagine if you will, the reports coming in to the busy Operations Centre and the identikit artists being assembled, a freshly blank painted wall has been prepared and as the witnesses supply the details, the artists begin to cover the walls with their impressions of the suspects.

Gradually, the wall fills up with figures and the details are refined until the police know exactly who they are looking for.

"There were police stations all over Egypt and that's why there are so many painted walls."

Henry had to admit that this was really intriguing and he found himself leaning forward as if trying to reach the details before the others could get to them.

Professor North gasped, "So, was it a success, did they catch everybody?"

Percy slumped "Unfortunately, no. By the time a wall had been plastered, whitewashed and all the figures had been painted on, even the Israelites had escaped."

The Archaeologists slowly glanced towards each other in turn as the timelines of the past tried desperately to align with the timelines of the present and make even a modicum of sense from the things they were hearing.

One of the female assistants decided on an exit strategy and announced, "I'd better go and prepare dinner or the chicken will be raw."

"Typical townie" snorted Arkle entering by the main door. "Chickens don't roar" she added, "At best they make a constipated clucking noise."

The Professors and their assistants sat in the tents where they had set up camp ready for a half-hearted exploratory trip in the morning and tried to make sense of the recent events.

117

Professor North still had the leaflet from Percy's welly and he carefully held it outside the tent flap every time he referred to it, it was the reference to a cave and paintings which disturbed him.

If it was there it should be easy to find, after all in a valley you only have to follow the walls around until you find a hole.

Geraldine was dangling from ropes again, but this time she had stolen a powerful torch from the mafia who had stolen it from Ronald. She had been really proud of herself, until Jasper charged an outrageous amount for the battery which led her to believe that she had been set up yet again. But anyway, here she was gently swinging on the rope Arkle had left secured for her.

Painted animals and stick-men hunters covered the walls in wonderful shades of ochre and black, but however much she squinted, she couldn't shake the impression that some of the cattle were wearing spectacles and some of the hunters were kicking a football.

Trying to peer through the leaping shadows, she laboriously swung herself closer and closer to the walls, and then she spotted the sweet wrappers.

Jasper hadn't seen much television or cinema, the lack of electricity had meant trips to the next valley and peering through windows or shouting "fire" and letting the stampede go by before finding a seat, sometimes people even left popcorn behind in their panic.

But, lack of experience or not, the crash of the bar room door and the sight of Geraldine alerted him to pure cinematic tension where the orchestra would be reaching a crescendo as the intruder stomped towards the victim.

"*What have you done?*" hissed Geraldine.

Jasper gave his orange juice a last insolent slurp and eyed the 'nut-job from the museum' warily, "It was Percy" he said.

Geraldine whirled round to catch any stray male from the Valley's population, but the bar was empty and when she turned back, Jasper had gone, leaving the faint click of a closing panel behind him.

Geraldine was torn between going to the Archaeologists and clearing up the misunderstanding, but that would mean that she was responsible for the Valley being taken over by outsiders and all her hard work at staying in complete obscurity would be wasted.

The alternative was allowing that clown Prince of a gardener to reveal all the same information by accident resulting in the same

118

outcome. She sighed, of all the things she hadn't studied (not officially anyway) was murder and yet the job always seemed to fall on her, "So be it," she thought and headed off for Cuthbert's farm.

Chapter Thirty-Seven

The cooking range was plinking away and the kettle was hissing, the atmosphere was warm and cloying and the men were at their leisure.

Jasper had tried to warn them, but they had smiled condescendingly, so he stole Ronald's knife and took up his place behind the pot plant.

As usual, when Percy was outside pottering in the barns, Cuthbert left an old football behind the door in case his friend had need to kick the door in and make the thatch slip like an ill-fitting wig.

This time though, it was Geraldine who burst in and promptly burst back out again as the door refused to be intimidated.

Staggering slowly back in, she muttered "Percy, kill Percy" whilst rubbing her nose.

The men stayed relaxed because it was obvious that they were safe and entertainment was afoot, especially when Percy came through the back door wiping his hands on an oily rag and asking "any tea left?"

The Archaeologists had been having a sing-song of old favourites like 'Sand gets in your eyes,' 'Only love me if you really dig me' and 'Mummy let's rock and roll' when they became aware of a strange smell creeping under the tent flap.

As it built up, the convivial evening was coming under threat, so Professor North ventured out to investigate.

This is when his female assistants really came into their own as he sent them out in front.

The source of the smell seemed to be a red and white striped tent nearby where a chorus even more raucous than their own was belting out "Drains, drains, drains, drains," repeatedly.

This had become a standard for the drains team because Buster wasn't good at remembering lyrics and the council was an equal opportunities employer.

This arduous singing had of course left one-lung Louie completely out of breath and Buster couldn't multi-task so it was left to swivelling Simon to answer the door, or flap in this case.

At first an arm came out holding a paraffin lamp which was fair enough but when Simon's head appeared with one eye swivelling wildly whilst trying to adjust to the darkness and the other giving the visitors a glassy appraisal the female assistants abandoned Professor North in a lemming like rush back to their own tent where there was a plentiful supply of shovels and they set up a perimeter.

The Drains Inspector replaced Simon at the flap and invited the Professor to join them, but the man wisely chose to sit outside and upwind as they discussed tomorrow's survey. It turned out that they were both following the general theory of following the Valley walls on the basis of 'There has to be a hole around here somewhere.'

Back in Cuthbert's kitchen, Geraldine was in full flow, she had screamed at Cuthbert for faking a Shakespearean play which brought them all here in the first place, she had screamed at Percy for everything she couldn't blame on Cuthbert and she had even screamed at a pot plant in the corner for drawing spectacles on cows.

Everyone else was transfixed, this was entertainment of the highest order, especially if you could remain a spectator, and the Captain, Henry and Ronald leant back and savoured the moment.

Geraldine was breathing heavily as she looked around the room, she hadn't been fooled by Jasper trying to blame Percy for the sheer juvenile vandalism of the spectacles and football, after all what sort of adult would be stupid enough to eat sweets shaped like pretend vegetables and then leave the wrappers everywhere?

At that moment Percy reached down into his welly and began to un-wrap a candy cucumber.

"You!" screamed Geraldine as Percy fled.

* * *

The morning dawned cold and the Archaeologists emerged from their tents and began to exercise and warm up, it could be a rigorous life out on a dig especially when the road gang had a roaring fire going and the smell of bacon cooking was chasing vegetarianism into a vague memory.

The surveyor, Cecil Carruthers was disgusted at the lack of professionalism involved in looking for the cave, but he had to admit that the bacon sandwich was more than making up for it.

His assistant was usually the butt of jokes and nudges and winks because his competence on 'air-guitar' using the striped survey pole, but today he was in his element because two of the female assistants had grabbed a shovel each and they had formed a trio.

Just as everyone was prepared to head off in various vague directions, Geraldine came walking slowly into the encampment and introduced herself to Professor North by saying,

"Good morning Professor, I am the local Archaeologist and museum curator, Geraldine," her outstretched hand was ignored as the Professor spluttered, "But the local man is Gerald Dean, I've met him, amazing anecdotes."

Geraldine glared and hissed "*Geraldine*, you nitwit not *Gerald Dean*. You met the local imbecile, Percy Plumm who spread those leaflets, just when everyone had decided to keep things a secret."

"What things?" asked the Professor craftily.

Geraldine's anger had made her careless and she found herself saying, "That cave for a start."

This of course wouldn't have been too bad, but she actually pointed to a depression marked by a distinctively shaped tree as she said it.

"The Professor patted her hand condescendingly and whispered, "Don't worry whoever you are, I'll tell Mr Dean what a great help you have been."

Then he shouted, "Forward everyone, my experiences and instincts tell me that our destination is very near."

Geraldine stood and gaped as everyone dutifully trooped passed her and followed him.

Percy was sat in the dark and he was fuming, his tractor was ticking over beneath him, so its exhaust was also fuming, in fact if it hadn't been for the hole in the top of the cave above him, all those combined fumes would have solved all Percy's problems for him, but as it was, a plume of smoke simply escaped through the trees above on top of the hill.

It had been bad enough being blamed for the mafia's art classes over the years and the abuse Geraldine had heaped upon his ancestors, but the final straw had been seeing the love of his life and his soul mate both playing air-guitar with that drip of a surveyor's assistant, just because Percy hadn't chosen between them yet, they were straying already. It was no wonder he preferred his plants.

The archaeologists were moving through the tunnel in single file and approaching the cave when one of the assistants stumbled and shone her torch downwards. Her shrieks caused everyone to gather around her staring in silence until an angry Professor North came storming back to rant about only causing a fuss when it was necessary but he too stood in shocked silence at the sight of the trail of three-toed footprints embedded in the rock of an old riverbed.

They continued towards the cave in a trance and even the Professor intoning into his voice recorder and taking all the credit for the find couldn't shake the feeling of great things to come.

Percy watched the lights approaching, he had heard everyone discussing how the buildings would be flattened and the Valley unoccupied for years and this simply did not fit in with his retirement plans which basically consisted of leeching off Cuthbert and blaming the mafia for everything, come to think of it, he was almost there.

The Archaeologists had become a random rabble of gasping sightseers, pointing and gasping in all directions. They had soon run out of adjectives and superlatives and everything was either "cool" or "awesome."

Professor North forced a temporary discipline and forced them all to concentrate their torch beams together and sweep across the walls in a methodical manner. "The Holy Grail." he muttered "My career is complete, I am ..."

He was interrupted by someone asking whether this Valley was volcanic. "Of course not" he snapped, but he had to admit that the floor had begun to shake and dust was dribbling from some of the ledges above them.

Percy increased the revs on his tractor engine causing Annie the dinosaur's head to swing in front of him; then he switched on the lights and let out the clutch.

The disciplined scene in front of him disintegrated into beams of light waving about everywhere, it was like searchlights in the blitz with only the roar of the diesel engine as a back drop.

The Archaeologists shone every light they had at the charging monstrosity bearing down on them, but even with their accumulated I.Q's the result was the same, they were being attacked by a dinosaur which had not only survived for millions of years, but it had evolved its own set of headlights as well.

The vibrations from Percy's tractor and the fact that he was bouncing about in some of the footprints meant that either the dinosaur head or its tail or the bulldozer blade on the front of the tractor was following quite an erratic course and pieces of cave wall were beginning to become part of the cave floor instead.

Professor North screamed soundlessly as a beautifully rendered Bison surrounded by hunters, landed at his feet only to be crunched into dust by a caterpillar track.

The Archaeologists charged back the way they had come and the Professor sat and cried as the ancient river bed was torn up before his eyes and spat out behind the dinosaur's tail.

Percy squinted as his machine broke out into the sunlight of the Valley, there was very little of Annie left. The head had been battered and was drooping under the tractor and the tail was just a series of dinosaur coloured ribbons trailing behind.

The population of the Valley was lined up to greet Percy, so he pushed his old flying goggles up on his head and beamed at his audience, whilst behind him, Professor North stumbled out into the fresh air just as the hill collapsed behind him leaving just a dip and a cloud of dust.

Professor North spotted P.C. Beeching, ran across and demanded that he "Arrest that man," pointing at Percy.

The officer smiled and took out his notebook, "With pleasure, sir" he said "on what charge?"

Professor North reeled, "Isn't it obvious man?" he demanded.

Beeching scratched under his helmet, "Not really sir, I can't arrest him for being Percy, because it's a unique occupation that is, so it's probably protected."

The Professor stared, "So he really is Percy Plumm? Then arrest him for impersonating Geraldine."

The officer couldn't hide his amazement, "Arrest him for impersonating a woman sir, in those wellies?"

Once again, the Professor felt his highly educated world tilt, "Arrest him for impersonating an Archaeologist then." The constable looked around at Percy, "But he hasn't," he said slowly, in case the man before him was in shock.

"Hasn't what?" spluttered North.

"Escaped," explained Beeching.

The Professor was seething, "What the devil are you talking about you buffoon; an Archaeologist, not an Escapologist."

The Constable closed his notebook very deliberately and replied, "You said he was an escapologist, but with my superior surveillance skills, I can see that he hasn't escaped at all, so all your evidence is a fabrication and seeing as I heard you say it, it's probably hearsay as well, so I'm arresting you for fabricating hearsay."

He then proceeded to turn around slowly in circles as he tried to reach the handcuffs out of reach on the back of his belt.

* * *

The ladies had been sat on a grassy knoll throughout all this with a gingham tablecloth and a picnic spread out before them. "Sorry about the tearoom Margery," said Elspeth patting the back of her friend's hand.

Margery smiled around her circle of friends as she replied, "Well girls, we're back where we started, but at least we started out on top eh?" she said, nodding towards the men, even Arkle smiled as she reached into the picnic basket.

Professor North had begun to regain his composure and he wasn't going to see his title as the man who found the dinosaurs thrown away, *nothing would move him from this spot,* but just at that moment a shadow fell across him, the ground shook and what seemed like a ton of tweed smelling of horse came charging towards him followed by a tomato with a smiley face rolling down the hill behind her. He fled.

~ The End ~

About the Author

Patrick Barrett is a sixty year old ex-miner from Mansfield in Nottinghamshire. He is married to Paula and between them, they have several children. 'Shakespeare's Cuthbert' was his first book, though he has been writing comedy for several years.

His aims as a writer are 'to be successful and make people laugh by providing them with an escape from the harshness of real life'.

His other abiding interest is in antiques.